C0-DKN-410

Library of
Davidson College

IRELAND

From the Act of Union • 1800
to the Death of Parnell • 1891

*Seventy-seven novels and collections
of shorter stories by twenty-two*
Irish and Anglo-Irish novelists

selected by

PROFESSOR ROBERT LEE WOLFF
Harvard University

A GARLAND SERIES

With Essex in Ireland

Emily Lawless

with an introduction by
Robert Lee Wolff

Garland Publishing, Inc., New York & London
1979

828
L418w

For a complete list of the titles in this series,
see the final pages of this volume.

Introduction copyright © 1979 by Robert Lee Wolff
All rights reserved

This facsimile has been made from a copy in
the Yale University Library (Ip.L484.890).

The volumes in this series are printed on acid-free,
250-year-life paper.

Library of Congress Cataloging in Publication Data

Lawless, Emily, Hon., 1845–1913.
With Essex in Ireland.

(Ireland, from the Act of Union, 1800,
to the death of Parnell, 1891)
Reprint of the 1890 ed. published by Smith, Elder, London.
1. Essex, Robert Devereux, earl of, 1567–1601—Fiction.
2. Ireland—History—1558–1603—Fiction.
I. Title. II. Series.
PZ3.L425Wi 1979 [PR4878.L6] 823 78-11884
ISBN 0-8240-3521-6

Printed in the United States of America

82-968

The Irish Fiction of
the Honourable Emily Lawless

Emily Lawless (1845–1913)[1] was the second child and
eldest daughter of the third Lord Cloncurry and so a
granddaughter of the second peer, who, as Valentine
Lawless, had been a sympathizer with the United
Irishmen of 1798 and an opponent of the Union with
England in 1800–1801. He was twice imprisoned. It
was his father who left the Catholic Church,
conformed to the Church of England, was elected to
Parliament, and was created first a Baronet (1776)
and then a Baron (1789). The family, then, were
relatively recent recruits to the Ascendancy. Emily
Lawless' mother was the beautiful Elizabeth Kirwan
of Castle Hackett, County Galway, who found herself
with full responsibility for their nine children when
her husband died in 1859. Emily was then fourteen.
Part of the year the family lived at Maretimo House,
the family residence near Dublin, and the rest of the
year in her mother's native Galway.

As a child, Emily Lawless was an avid reader and
enjoyed memorizing long passages of Elizabethan
plays. Once when her father asked her to give her
latest recitation to an evening party of his fellow
sporting squires, she obliged by declaiming a long
blank verse diatribe delivered by a husband to his

v

faithless wife, in which each line ended with the word *whore,* a word she liked but of whose meaning she had not the faintest idea. The gentlemen did, however, and enjoyed the performance until her father gently turned her off ("Thank you, Emily; very nice, but that is enough"). But her real passion was for nature. She became an excellent amateur entomologist and botanist. In *Traits and Confidences* (1897; No. 75 in this series) will be found an entertaining reminiscence of her pursuit (aged ten) of a rare moth. Miss Lawless' accurate observation of the Irish landscape and of the sea in all seasons and all weathers became a notable feature—unobtrusive but immensely effective—of her fiction, when she began to write in the early 1880's under friendly prompting from the successful and enormously prolific Scottish novelist Mrs. Oliphant. Her first fiction was set in England, but it was her Irish stories that made her famous in her lifetime and deserve revival now.

Hurrish. A Study (2 vols., Edinburgh, 1886; No. 71) was her third novel and the first about Ireland. Set in the region known as the Burren, a beautiful portion of the Atlantic coast in northern County Clare, where the landscape appears desolate, but rich grass growing amidst the rocks provides good fodder for sheep and cattle, *Hurrish* tells the story of a peasant. Hurrish is a good man and a peaceful one, whose mother, a fierce old harridan, feels "shame" because her son is so averse to violence, but who nonetheless kills and is killed in circumstances wholly Irish and entirely convincing. His family—including his children, his gentle virtuous sister-in-law, even his dog—all ring true, as do the parish priest and the village idiot. Of course, Miss Lawless was looking at the peasantry from outside; about that she had no choice. But her understanding and sympathy seem to have been boundless.

In the 1880's, with Land League agitation rising and replacing the activities of the secret societies so often encountered in the earlier fiction in this series, we find Hurrish scorning and detesting the "Land-grabbers," the new men who have profited by the Encumbered Estates Act to acquire land. But he still retains a "sneaking regard" for the "ould stock, the aboriginal landlord, so to speak," men like Pierce O'Brien, who resides on his estates, who does not press for his rents, who takes personal care of everything about his property, but who is nonetheless widely detested just because he *is* a landowner. Miss Lawless' depiction of O'Brien and of the sad fate he incurs because of the greed of other men serves as a late commentary on the practicality of Edgeworthian principles: Maria Edgeworth would have wholly approved of O'Brien and found herself unable to understand the circumstances that had rendered her precepts invalid. The farrier, Phil Rooney ("a finished gentleman if self-respect and the most perfect breeding in the world are the essentials"), can remember the Famine and, of course, the failure of Fenianism. Like Hurrish, he too has no use for "the modern generation of agitators."

But Hurrish and Rooney are almost alone now, "like the elk or the old Irish wolf-hound," says Miss Lawless, reverting to the symbols of Irish antiquity used by the novelists since Maria Edgeworth. The newer generation, half-educated, with Americanized aspirations, form a wholly different breed. In the end, Hurrish must die because "Hate of the Law is the birthright and the dearest possession of every native son of Ireland ... because for many a year that country had been as ill-governed a morsel of earth as was to be found under the wide-seeing eye of God." *Hurrish* appeared in 1886, the year of Gladstone's effort to put through Irish Home Rule, and of its failure amidst rising agrarian discontent. Everybody was thinking about Ireland. *Hurrish* gave the public a new and sympathetic and knowledgeable view of some of the major Irish problems, while emphasizing past English misgovernment and neglect. *Hurrish* was widely hailed and Miss Lawless' next novel eagerly awaited.

After a competent one-volume history of Ireland (1887), she published *With Essex in Ireland* (1890; No. 72), ostensibly a firsthand account written as a journal by a participant in the Earl of Essex' expedition to Ireland in 1599 as Queen Elizabeth I's Lord Lieutenant. Essex' mission was to subdue Hugh O'Donnell, the rebellious Earl of Tyrone. The diarist, Essex' secretary, Henry Harvey, writing in pleasant Elizabethan prose, records Essex' march from Dublin southwest to Cahir and the return to Dublin by a roughly parallel route lying south and east of the outward journey, followed by a sortie northwards into Louth and a meeting with O'Donnell. So convincingly did Miss Lawless do her work as an imitator of Elizabethan style that many of her readers were convinced that she had discovered and edited an important new document, instead of writing a historical novel. Even Mr. Gladstone, learned man, student of Ireland, and inveterate novel reader though he was, was taken in. When he found out the truth, he was all the more excited and piqued. He could not wait to meet Emily Lawless and knocked on her hotel room door while she was staying at Cannes. She was lying on her bed with her shoes off and in her dressing gown, and thought the knock was that of a waiter bringing her tea. Horribly embarrassed at being discovered slightly dishevelled by the three-times Prime Minister, she was delighted when he sat down in her room and talked to her uninterruptedly for two hours about Ireland.[2]

With Essex in Ireland, sticking closely to the facts of sixteenth-century history, is also a pointed commentary on the entire disastrous history of Anglo-Irish relations. Among the fierce Elizabethan Englishmen, sure of their superiority to the wild Irish, Essex and the diarist, Henry Harvey, emerge as decent and relatively humane. Gradually their experiences teach them that the Irish are more than savages, bearers of a Celtic culture that the Englishmen cannot understand but that leaves them in awe. It is easy to understand, therefore, how greatly the book appealed to Yeats, who in 1895 included it in his list of the thirteen best books of Irish fiction.[3] Miss Lawless herself later said of it, "The true hero, or rather heroine, is the wretched country itself, groaning under its troubles, and yet with that curious fascination which we all feel," and added that it was her favorite among her own books, since she was able to imagine that it was *not* by her.[4] A modern reader is likely to share Yeats's view of it.

Grania. The Story of an Island (2 vols., 1892; No. 73)

is set on Inishmaan, the middle island of the three Aran islands in Galway Bay, opposite the Burren, scene of *Hurrish*. Here life is even simpler and starker. The time of the action—the 1860's—has no particular importance; unlike *Hurrish, Grania* is not a novel in which political considerations play a role. The infertile, storm-swept, and often fogbound rock, to which a few inhabitants cling, is a universe in itself, within which Miss Lawless introduces only three chief characters: Grania, her sister, and her suitor. The changing of the seasons and the vicissitudes of the weather provide the events that govern their lives. The two incidents in which the outside world impinges—a visit to the Galway fair and the momentary landing of three tourists on the island—serve only to emphasize Grania's isolation. Her fate is pure tragedy made the more poignant by her own realization that it is inevitable. Reflection on what might have happened had Miss Lawless given her plot a different turn suggests that the tragedy—which Grania herself fully understands—would only have been more protracted and more agonizing.

None of the personages ordinarily speaks in English, so Miss Lawless does not give them a brogue. Instead she "translates" their Irish speech into a musical form of English that effectively suggests the difference between the two languages. Published six years before J. M. Synge's first visit to the Aran Islands and ten before his fourth, *Grania* as a novel challenges comparison with his celebrated journal, *The Aran Islands,* based on these sojourns. When *Grania* appeared, Miss Lawless received letters of praise from Viscount Morley, who compared her to

George Sand; from W. E. H. Lecky, historian of eighteenth-century Ireland, who became a close friend; from George Meredith; and from her admirer, Gladstone, now Prime Minister for the fourth and last time. Swinburne wrote her that he found it "one of the most exquisite and perfect works of genius in the language—unique in pathos, humour, and convincing persuasion of truthfulness."[5]

Two years after *Grania* came *Maelcho* (2 vols., 1894; No. 74), a second grim historical novel of sixteenth-century Ireland, set in the years 1579–1582, about two decades before Essex' expedition. The scene is Connaught and Munster, the protagonist an English youth who escapes a massacre of his noble Irish relatives by their Irish enemies and flees to Iar Connaught, the domain of the wild O'Flahertys. The description of tribal life in this desolate region south of Connemara is extremely well done. From this dangerous refuge, the hero escapes a second time southward into the hands of the Spaniards and Irish noble rebels against Elizabeth who are invading Kerry, and finally makes his way into the forces of the Elizabethan armies sent to restore order to the southwest. This they try to accomplish by wholesale murder and devastation, described in all its grisly horror.

Maelcho himself is the *seanachie* (historian, harper, bard, magician, influential counsellor) of Sir James Fitzmaurice, one of the "Geraldine" Irish rebels, relatives of the Earl of Desmond. The reader meets Maelcho only when he is already an old man, and the novel suffers from our having to take on faith the assurances of the influence and power he had wielded in his earlier life. Once he has been introduced, moreover, Miss Lawless divides her attention between him and her young English protagonist, so that the structure of the novel is flawed. Her portrait of the sinister Cormac Cas, *seanachie* of the O'Flahertys, tells us more about the role of the minstrel-adviser in Celtic tribal Ireland. There is also a vivid account of the mendicant friars, lineal predecessors of Carleton's Darby Moore in "The Midnight Mass" (*Traits and Stories, Second Series,* 3 vols., 1833; No. 35) and of the other mendicants that throng his pages. When Yeats expanded his February 1895 list of thirteen best Irish works of fiction to sixteen later in the year, he included *Maelcho*, which he had just read, giving Miss Lawless the same number of titles as the Banims. Only Carleton had more.[6]

Emily Lawless' last completed work of adult fiction about Ireland was the collection called *Traits and Confidences* (1897; No. 75) which included the auto-biographical essay on her girlhood moth hunt, "An Entomological Adventure." Two tales of assassination, one set in 1798, the other contemporary with the book's appearance, a brief medieval romance, memories and a story of the Famine, and a tale of tragic mésalliance that ends—almost too late—in reconciliation make up a varied and a delightful small book, less finished than the longer fiction but no less arresting. *The Race of Castlebar* (1913) she did not complete. Shan Bullock finished it for her and supplied most of its Irish portion. We therefore do not republish it here. In addition to her fiction, she wrote a life of Maria Edgeworth (1904); *Gilly*, a children's book (1906); and several books of verse, including *The Wild Geese* (1902) and *The Point of View* (1909), a small volume published privately for the aid of the Galway fishermen. The University of Dublin gave her the honorary degree of D. Litt. in 1905.

Emily Lawless was a deeply patriotic Irishwoman, much influenced in her thinking by her cousin Sir Horace Plunkett (1854–1932), younger son of the sixteenth Lord Dunsany, who in his young manhood spent a decade ranching in Wyoming, and after some preliminary efforts founded the Irish Agricultural Organization Society in 1894, in support of agricultural reform, notably cooperatives. Its organ, the *Irish Homestead*, founded in 1895, to which George William Russell (AE) contributed and which he later edited, also published some of Emily Lawless' verse. A great admirer of AE, who after 1897 was one of the I.A.U's chief organizers and helped the cooperative movement grow in ten years to the number of 876 societies and an annual turnover of £3,000,000, Plunkett was a Unionist in politics. He was a Member of Parliament after 1895, and the moving spirit behind the Land Act of 1896 and the creation of the Department of Agriculture and Technical Instruction for Ireland. With his later successes and disappointments we need not deal here.[7] Emily Lawless took her lead from him. She did not believe Ireland was ready for Home Rule, but did criticize British policy sharply. This explains why some nationalists accused her of being "unfair" to the Irish peasant characters in her novels, and some conservatives accused her of being "unfair" to British Rule. In 1911 she wrote Plunkett that a leading member (whom she does not name) of the "Gaelic Theatre and circle" had written her that what she had written had "helped them." "I am not *anti-Gaelic* at all," she commented to Plunkett, "as long as it is only Gaelic *enthuse* and does not include politics."[8]

The last years of her life she spent in England, increasingly an invalid, still happy working in her garden, "a tall, almost angular" woman in an "almost shapeless gardening hat," intelligent, warm-hearted, open-minded, with a multitude of friends, intensely Irish.

Robert Lee Wolff

Notes

1. Emily Lawless does not appear in the *DNB:* clearly an oversight. The entry on her in *The New Cambridge Bibliography of English Literature,* III, 2nd edition (Cambridge: University Press, 1969), col. 1907, among "Anglo-Irish Poets," includes an unusually large number of errors; her first book, *The Chelsea Householder,* appeared in London in 1882 in three volumes; *Hurrish* (No. 71) originally was published in two volumes; *Major Lawrence, F.L.S.* (1888) was published in three volumes; and there are two separate entries, both garbled, for *With Essex in Ireland* (No. 72), the first edition of which is the 1890 Smith, Elder edition reproduced in this series. In the absence of any biographical study, the obituary in the *Times,* October 23, 1913, is useful; so is Edith Sichel, "Emily Lawless," *The Nineteenth Century,* LXXVI (July 1914), 80–100. It too has a good many inaccuracies, however.

2. Sichel, p. 86. Gladstone would become Prime Minister for the fourth time in 1892.

3. Stephen Marcus, *Yeats and the Beginning of the Irish Renaissance* (Ithaca and London: Cornell University Press, 1970), p. 285.

4. Sichel, p. 86.

5. Sichel, p. 85. This letter is not included in C.Y. Lang's six-volume edition of Swinburne's letters.

6. Marcus, p. 286.

7. See F. S. L. Lyons, *Ireland Since the Famine* (London; Weidenfeld and Nicolson, 1971), pp. 202–211 and *passim*.

8. Sichel, p. 87.

WITH ESSEX IN IRELAND

WITH ESSEX IN IRELAND

BEING EXTRACTS FROM A DIARY KEPT IN IRELAND
DURING THE YEAR 1599 BY MR HENRY HARVEY,
SOMETIME SECRETARY TO ROBERT DEVEREUX, EARL
OF ESSEX. WITH A PREFACE BY JOHN OLIVER
MADDOX, M.A. INTRODUCED AND EDITED

BY

HON. EMILY LAWLESS

AUTHOR OF 'HURRISH, A STUDY' ETC.

LONDON

SMITH, ELDER, & CO., 15 WATERLOO PLACE

1890

[All rights reserved]

The Preface

---◆◆---

WHETHER the following Relation doth in ought conduce to a real Knowledge of what befel during the short and troublous Government of Robert Devereux Earl of Essex in Ireland, let the Fit Reader judge. Something natheless it may be well to add, seeing that the aforesaid Relation is both faulty in Construction, and singularly abrupt in Conclusion. For the Writer of it he was born in Northwich, of an Ancient and Honourable Family, and early entered the Household of that Nobleman whom he followed. For Education he was brought up at the Universitie of Cambridge, where he misspent not his Time, but acquired a sound Knowledge of the Mathematicks and other solid Attainments, yet was ever most inclined to stray into the Flowerie Paths of Apolio, and is the Author of a Poem entitled 'VIOLANTILLA, OR THE MIRROR OF NOBILITIE,' which though not of that Durable Stuff like to survive to a Deathless Immortalitie, yet hath a sweet Delectableness, conjoined to a seemly

*Simplicitie of Diction both rare and delightsome to list to.
He was still in Ireland when those Events befel which
terminated in the Death of that Unhappy Nobleman
whom he followed, which last Event happening before he
could reach him, and thus tender even such Sorry Comfort
as might accrue from his Presence, so affected him that he
was for a while like to have died. Recovering presently,
he left England, and entered the Household of the Elector
Palatine, in which Prince's Service he expired in the
Twelfth Year of the Reign of our late Sovereign King
James of Blessed Memory.*

*For his Work now first printed, though it sufficiently
testifieth to the great Love he bore to his Unhappy Patron,
we might wish that it had been tempered throughout with
a nicer Discretion, more especially in those Portions which
relate to what took place in the Castle of Askeaton in
Munster, and at the passage of the Lagan in Ulster, which
Portions be, I must plainly avow, contrary in my Opinion
both to Religion and Firm Reason. With which Observation I leave the Right Worshipful Reader to sup from
it such Entertainment as he may.*

*His Majesty's and the said Right Worshipful Reader's
Servant to Command*

   JOHN OLIVER MADDOX M.A.

*From my Lodging in the Black Friars at London,
this 17th day of January* 1638

The Kingdome of IRELAND Devided into Fower PROVINCES Lemster, Munster, Ulster & Connagh.

London, Stanford's Geog'l Estab.

WITH ESSEX IN IRELAND

————◆————

I

Two days we lay at Beau Morris, the weather being very foul, the winds continuing ever at the North-ward and North Westward, from which points it were not possible for us to seize Dublin. Upon the third day we embarked, yet so fierce was still the sea and so violent the storm that her Majesty's pinnaces could scarce approach the land, the waves being lifted high in air, and falling with a great noise and roaring clamour upon the rocks. Very unlike were we to that gallant company which rode forth scarce two weeks earlier from my Lord's lodgings in Seething Lane, the people standing in crowds along Grace-church Street and Cornhill, yea pressing exceeding to behold his Lordship, crying aloud 'God save the Lord Essex! May God preserve the good

Earl!' the sun the while shining bright, and our hearts lifted with joy and pride to be of so great and mighty a company.

Nevertheless I remember that when we had got past Iseldon [1] the sky which had hitherto been clear suddenly became overcast, loud thunderings breaking forth, and great hail falling like stones descending from Heaven, whereat some of us grew pale, fearing that it betokened an evil issue of this our Enterprise. Only the Earl himself would hear of no such forebodings, saying that none but they that were of a sorry and doubtful stomach were moved out of their constancy by ought that the winds or sky could do, and so he continued throughout the whole journey, the latter portion of which was the worst that I in any country have encountered, more especially in that passage of the Welsh mountains called in their tongue Pen-men-Maure—a dreadful and savage mass of rocks rising up in the midst of the Queen's highway, most shocking to contemplate, and of great danger and impediment for those that have to travel on horseback across its declivities.

Now of the thirteen hours which we spent on board ship, and of the miseries endured therein

[1] Islington.

I will say nothing, for the remembrance of them is still grievous to me, as unto most of those that bore us company. For I remarked that the pangs of this sickness spared not even those that were of highest station, great Earls like my Lords of Southhampton and Rutland lying prostrate upon the deck in sore travail both of body and mind, even as did they that were of lower birth and station. For this sickness is like Death itself, and is a great and mighty Leveller, breaking down those partitions which God hath himself set and ordained between man and man.

Towards morning the wind however somewhat abated, and, the waves being less powerful, the pitching motions of the vessel became likewise less violent, so that I, leaving that place where I had lain all night, crawled upward upon the deck, being in very miserable plight, and cramped and stiff in every joint as I had been racked for many hours by orders of her Majesty's Star chamber. I had not stood there more than some ten minutes before the door of a small cabin which was to the right of me opened and his Lordship my Lord of Essex—or rather his Excellency the Lord Lieutenant of Ireland as I must henceforth learn to call him—stepped out from the

place consigned to him during the voyage.
Seeing me he turned toward where I stood beside
the taffrail, clinging by my two hands to a rope
which depended from some portion of the furniture
of the vessel.

'Ha Hal,' quoth he, 'art stirring already, my
good sonneteer?' (so it was often his Lordship's
pleasure to call me.)   'Nay but thou lookest sadly
for a poet,' he added, 'and of a green and right
dolorous countenance!'

With that he came forward, as his way is, and
laid his hand in friendly fashion upon my shoulder.
Whereat I would willingly have responded in suitable terms for his courtesy and gracious conde-
scension, but could in no wise do so, being in truth
in very evil case, and little stable upon my lower
limbs, which seemed to belong rather to some
other person than to myself, giving way below me
at every lurching movement of the vessel.

Seeing how it was with me his Lordship
smiled, and so turned away, and began to walk to
and fro upon the deck, himself of a very ruddy
and cheerful countenance, and moving with a free
and lusty step, at which I marvelled greatly,
being astonished how anyone could preserve his
balance in that unstable equilibrium.   But indeed

his powers exceed those of all men, upon sea no less than on land, and in those matters which are small and light no less than in·those which are of a great and weighty import!

At that time the sea was still covered with great waves of a dull greenish colour, having upon their tops small portions of white, like to women's coifs, the sky too still overcast with clouds, moving over the whole eastern expanse of it. In the extreme west there was nevertheless a pale line visible, which was the first harbinger of that Land of Ireland towards which we were making, and beyond it a faint redish glow seemed to be reflected in the sky, as though a candle or indifferent lantern had been placed near it.

Seeing this his Excellency stopped short, and gazed at it very earnestly for the space of some six minutes, like one that discerned more therein than could be seen by mortal eyes.

'Methinks our Kingdom is lighting up in celebration of our coming!' said he to me, smiling and turning a little, like one that expected a cheerful answer.

Whereat, alas! I would again gladly have responded in meet terms, but could in no wise do so, my stomach being at the moment so sore disturbed, that with grief and pain I was obliged to refrain from speech altogether.

Now there had come up to the deck just then a young lad called Francis Gardner, the son of a widow lady of great virtue, and of a considerable estate in Somersetshire, which estate upon attaining his majority he himself was to inherit. But when first the talk began of the great company that my Lord of Essex was gathering together for the subjugation of the rebels in Ireland, the lad was mad to be allowed to go ; saying that rather than not do so he would serve the Earl as a horse boy ; whereat his mother with tears did long refuse him, declaring that she had been forewarned in dreams that if he went he would in no case ever return to her again.

But I, (being over persuaded by the lad, having known him from the hour of his birth, and ever loving and cherishing him even as a young brother) took upon me, as I now see foolishly, to intercede with the lady, saying that I would be answerable for his safety, and, further to reassure her, I told her that these Irish rebels would never dare assault us, we being in such great strength, and my Lord of Essex—my Lord Lieutenant that was to be—so tried and so terrible a soldier. And in this way with many tears and reluctantly she consented, seeing that the boy's heart was so set upon it that being thwarted in his wish, the grief and disappointment thereof might have worked him some lasting injury.

He, standing by, spake up boldly now in my Lord's presence, declaring that it was right and meet for Ireland thus to light her lamps in honour of his coming. 'For sure' cried he, 'the Jade knoweth well that he who approaches her is the One destined before all men to win her from her savagery, and to bring her to an understanding of those things that pertain to her welfare!'

'Beshrew thee lad, 'tis to be hoped thou speak'st by the book there!' said his Lordship smiling, and his face shone, as it doth when his soul is lit with great and noble thoughts. 'Methinks as we draw near I could e'en leap into the waves as they say the Roman general Julius did, and so come sooner to land,' quoth he, still smiling. And then he stood awhile, looking at that small light in the far distance, and we two beside him, silent also, feeling that he were best pleased so.

'Nathless yon hath been a ditch into which every great and goodly reputation, since ever a Lord Deputy, or a Lord Lieutenant came to its shores has fallen and been lost,' said he presently, yet rather as it seemed to himself than to us who stood by.

'The more Glory to him that is first to break through that evil spell!' cried young Gardner boldly.

At which I was both proud and astonished to hear the boy speak so well, yet would have checked him nevertheless for his forwardness, as unbecoming a youth of his years in speaking to one set in station so high above him. But my Lord—that is to say his Excellency the Lord Lieutenant of Ireland—turned and looked at him with a kindly eye, as if pleased with his spirit and daring. In truth he is a gallant lad, of an open ruddy and joy-inspiring countenance, such as it lifts the heart to look at. Neither is his Excellency one that would with sour looks repel those that wait upon him, preferring ever love to a more cold and dolorous service.

He, turning presently away, set to walking again, leaving the lad and myself standing where we were beside the taffrail. And as he walked I noted that he cast eyes of eagerness towards that land we were approaching, so that one who had seen him so walking and so looking, and wist not who it was, would have said—' Surely this is some great Lord who goes to meet that Lady whom he loveth?' Neither would they have greatly erred in so saying, for his Excellency, who is more of a poet both by nature and execution than many who profess themselves of that rhyming craft, oft spake in my hearing of this Land of Ireland as if she were in truth a woman, one who was froward, and had done many things contrary to order and reasonableness, being led away by those that would betray her to her own undoing, and yet withal not without much faithfulness of nature, who, were her affections once secured, might follow him whom she loved to the world's end.

And I who know his inmost thoughts, being so near to him—not merely in service, but also in the nearer and tenderer relations of the heart— know that in accepting this governance he was moved, less by pride and worldly ambition, which they who know him not are ever ready to impute (judging his nobler heart by their own covetous ones) but by the thought of bringing back this land, which has strayed so far from civility, and leading her as a meet and a docile handmaiden unto our Queen and Mistress. Which thing, little like as, alas! it seems now to come to pass, might, it appears to me, have in very deed and truth

been accomplished but for those envious malign-
ings whose foul and evil mission seems ever to be
on the watch to bring to naught all noble enterprise. Yea our royal Mistress did herself hold
it to be not impossible, else had she never granted
to my Lord such powers and authority, as were
never given to any other Viceroy only to him
alone. ' Having '—as she herself said—' cast eyes
on all her servants, and chosen him before all
others, out of former experience of his faith, valour,
wisdom, and extraordinary merit.'

By ten of the clock we sailed into the bay of
Dublin. The tide nevertheless being low we were
forced to lie out midway between the Head of
Howthe and the mainland, the river being largely
closed in, especially towards the north bank, with
a great quantity of sand, and the water over it
exceeding shallow. We landed at last in small
boats or shallops at a place called the *Ring's End*,
which is about a mile or less from the walls of
the city.

Here his Excellency was met by the Lords
Justices, also the Mayor, and Sheriffs, with the
Pensioners, Captains, and other gentlemen, to the

number of some five hundred horse, very fitly caparisoned, though somewhat scant methought in the matter of arms. They, receiving him upon his setting foot on land, set up loud acclamations, as though a very King or God had come amongst them, each endeavouring so to pass before the other that he might be the first to tender his obedience. All which his Excellency, receiving graciously, did with many courteous terms reply to; yea even we in our degree were constrained to utter many words of civility and satisfaction, which to speak truth we would fain in our hearts have refrained from, being still so sad and sore by reason of the buffeting of the waves.

Then, when all were debarked, we set forth from the water's edge, his Excellency riding Suleiman, his best-esteemed charger, and wearing a suit of plain armour, but over it a surcoat of white, richly embroidered in flowers, with hose of velvet and riding boots of dark Spanish leather. There were not many along the road, save those already of our own company, and those few chiefly of the baser sort, who stared upon us with open mouths, stupid as sheep, or, if they louted, louting with a sullen and timorous aspect, like men who paid obedience, not from pleasure, but for very fear's

sake ; which louting nevertheless whenever my Lord
perceived he with courteous gesture plucked from
his head his own plumed hat, and doffed it in
response, whereat the poor fools stared the more,
being as it seemed but little used to the like
courteous and comely behaviour.

After about half an hour's going, through ways
so foul that the worst in England would have
been fair by comparison, we arrived at the walls of
the city, which are of a considerable height from
the ground, and set about with stoutish towers at
intervals.   Here the keys of the city were pre-
sented to his Excellency, which he, receiving in
the name of her Majesty, did with gracious words
restore unto the custody of the most worshipful the
Lord Mayor.

When the gates were flung open, and we had
ridden inside, in place of that vacancy through
which we had passed we found ourselves suddenly
in the midst of a great crowd and turmoil of people,
pressed closely together as you may see pilchards
collected for packing.   Whom at first I took to
be gathered because of the coming of his Excellency, but after a while found to be general over
the city, being made up of all that had fled
hither for safety, there being since the late lament-

able disaster and triumph of the rebels no safety anywhere for the Queen's poor lieges, save only in walled towns. Yea, even the Earl of Ormonde, who until my Lord's coming did bear chief rule in this kingdom, hath for many weeks remained grievously pent in his own castle of Kilkenny, not daring for lack of force to take the field against those traitors, who, being thus feared, have waxed more and more bold in their insolence, believing that none in all this realm durst gainsay them.

When therefore his Excellency appeared, the troops which had also debarked following him, and the banners flying and all the Lords and knights that had come over in his company riding behind and on either side, there arose a shout the like of which I have never heard. All that were near the gate pressing forward to meet us with cries of welcome, the tears running over their eyes, and falling down upon their cheeks, the women holding up their babes to see us, nay scarce were they to be refrained from throwing themselves under the horse's feet, so joyed were they to behold him whom they did account as their Saviour. These as I afterwards learnt were mainly of English birth and breeding, being for the most part made up of

those who with difficulty had escaped out of
Munster, having been set upon there with great
fury by the rebels, who having aforetime possessed
all that province, esteemed this in their frowardness and wickedness to be a good time to repossess
themselves of the same.

Finding that the Castle of Dublin, which is the
chief seat of governance, had since the late Lord
Borough's time become unfit for habitation by reason
of the damp and neglect, in place of going there,
my Lord alighted at the house of one Mr. Usher, a
gentleman of some reputation, possessing a good new
house close by the Bridge's foot, which house had
also several times been slept in by the late Lord
Deputy Borough and Sir William Russell on their
first arrival.   The same Mr. Usher, being amongst
those that came to meet his Excellency, had, as we
approached the town, parted company with us, and
spurred on ahead so as to be in readiness to greet
his Excellency on the threshold.   Which he did,
having beside him also two fair damsels, whom I
took at first to have been his daughters, and
marvelled greatly, perceiving them so little to re-
semble one another.   Next day, coming to know
them better, I discovered that one of them was a
cousin, being in fact a ward, and orphaned of both

her parents. Fairer gentlewomen I have rarely
seen, and rejoiced within myself to behold such
comely flowers blooming in so sad and waste a
soil. In figure the daughter of Mr. Usher was of
middle height, of a willow-like grace, her hair fair,
and so fine that it seemed under her coif to be
of spun silk, her eyes like unto those of a dove,
and her name, as I presently learnt, Agatha, which
seemed to me made to suit one of so sweet and
gentle an aspect. Whereas the other, who was
called Mistress Bridget, was of a ruddier colour
and more daring carriage, having eyes of a dark
grey, with lashes extraordinarily thick, through
which they shone with wayward gleams as doth
the sun upon a storm-tossed sea. Her other features were of less noteable aspect, the nose rather
short, yet not displeasingly so, the mouth large
but of a good shape, and the teeth of a whiteness
which when she showed them seemed to sort well
with that flashing of the eyes of which I have
spoken.

For the Castle of Dublin methinks a fouler
place, fitter for holding her Majesties prisoners,
(whereof it containeth at the present time many
score), and less fit for the habitation of one
who stands in her own stead I have never

seen.   What struck me most upon approaching
it was the great number of heads and other
portions of rebels with which it was as it were
garnished.   For not alone were they set over the
main gateway [which is the natural and proper
place for the heads and limbs of traytors to be
disposed, and in which place we in England are
used to behold them], but fastened on rude
painted stakes set along the front of the Castle,
and upon the parapets, yea and in front of the
windows.   Which same appeared to me a foolish,
and even a somewhat barbarous and unhandsome
custom.   Neither were they as I was told of
any great or noted rebels, but for the most part
sorry knaves, sent in from the borders of the Pale
and elsewhere, O'Dempsys, O'Byrnes, and such like.
The chiefest of them being that Feagh Mac Hugh
O'Bryne, who was killed two years since in the
time of Sir William Russell, a somewhat notable
rascal, who did give the government in his time
no slight trouble.

His Excellency himself was ill pleased I observed at this sight, and averted his head, as
if sickened by the contemplation of so much
dead flesh, he being at all times loathe to look
upon such Trophies of Death, even where the

same when alive were his own or the Queen's enemies.

Inside the Castle is very dark, the windows small, and the glass green, and not clear. The furnishing very poor, such hangings as there are being mostly half pulled down and torn, as they had been roughly plucked by some rude hand, the whole so foul, uncared for, and unhandsome that it were a pity to look at. It was with the greater satisfaction therefore, the business which brought him to it being accomplished, that his Excellency and we who were to share his lodging returned to Mr. Usher's house, which is of a fair size and well furnished, the best in this respect of any house I have encountered in Ireland, with the exception of my Lord of Ormonde's at Kilkenny, and another castle, the property of Sir Walter Raleigh, at present in the charge of one Mr. Pine.

Both during his ride to the Castle and on his return to Mr. Usher's house—after being sworn in and having received the Council—his Excellency was accompanied by a great press of knights and gentlemen, all eager to do him honour, who with much fair seeming and many civil words assured him of the great joy they esteemed it to see one

C

of his fame and prowess as a soldier arrive to take command of this realm, which has of late suffered so much and sustained such injury, especially at the hands of that Arch rebel, and Fell Tyrant Tyrone; who has wasted the land at his pleasure, finding none to oppose him, but who being met by so approved a soldier as his Excellency, would doubtless now, they said, speedily bite the dust in shame and humiliation.

Nevertheless, even on this first day of our coming, I perceived some whose looks pleased me little, and from whom I augured small good, though with the rest they endeavoured to greet his Excellency with all fair seeming. Amongst which I might number no less than four which be of the very Irish Council itself, yet will I forbear, not through favour, or from fear of ought that any man may say of me, but through reverence simply of their places' sake.

II

NEXT morning, being the 9th day of May of
this year 1599, finding that his Excellency had
for the moment no occasion of my services, I
proposed to sally forth, and see such things as
are deemed worthiest of note in this town of
Dublin. Hearing of my determination the two
damsels, the daughter of Mr. Usher and her
cousin, offered to be my guides, saying they
would themselves show me such things as I ought
to see; which offer I with many humble thanks
right joyfully and gratefully accepted.

Leaving the house we set forth therefore from
the Bridge's foot, keeping close along the city
wall, one side of which here toucheth the yardway
of Mr. Usher, from which yardway to the Bridge
gate is, as I was told, one hundred and four feet
long, and the wall itself nineteen feet high and
four thick. At this place the wall encounters
the river Liffey, which at very full tide floweth

against it, but at other times leaves bare a wide space, of somewhat evil aspect and odour. Turning southward we next passed up Bridge Street, through sundry narrow streets or rather lanes, till we came to what is called the New gate, though now very old, and sorely in need of repair, and so past St. Nicholas Church, where we again met the city wall, it being drawn in a tight circle round about the town, the whole less than one English mile, as I was informed, from point to point, and leaving many houses upon the outside utterly naked and unprotected.

Here we ascended one of the watch towers, whence a general view of the city was, the damsels said, to be obtained, as indeed I found, although the houses being close to us upon all sides somewhat impeded the prospect. Worse built houses I have rarely seen, the roofs of no two seeming to slope in the same direction ; the walls in many places propped in strange fashion with poles and sticks, so that they most resembled a company of cripples, every man leaning for support upon his neighbour's arm.

That the town nevertheless stands well, and has a fair prospect I deny not. To the Eastward the bay is of a fine open shape, though a good

deal shut in to the Northward by the Head of
Howthe (the same promontory we coasted the
day before) while on the other side rises a range
of hills of a fair acclivity and very green to
look at. That these hills are of more plague
than profit to the town folk, is however I take
it plain, being waste ground, full of bogs, and
rocks, which none inhabit save O'Byrnes, O'Tooles,
and such like Fry of Satan, which same continually make incursions upon the town, so that
even up to its gates men are constrained to hold
their cattle in their hands, else are they of a
surety driven away by the like arrant thieves and
cattle lifters, these hilly places being but too apt
to bring forth such unpleasant fruit.

Of nearer objects the chief was the Castle
of Dublin, which, though mean and uncomely
upon a closer view, wears from a distance a fair
and substantial aspect, being quadrangular in
shape, and well garnished with towers, the chief
of which is called the Birmingham tower, the
roof of it steep and beset with windows, giving
light to rooms used for the safe keeping of state
prisoners.

What at this distance most attracted my at
tention was that upon the topmost point of al-

running as it were into the very blue of the sky,
stands a tall and white-painted stake, upon which,
as I had already been informed of the knowing,
it is the custom to set up the head of any Chief
Rebel newly slain, which head remains there aloft
in air till either it fall to pieces by natural decay,
or till a yet greater than he be slain.   And being
so set, atop of all other things living and dead in
the city, and having naught above it but the sky
itself, and the birds of the air, or by night the stars
shining so cold and clear, it is in waggery of the
citizens called ' THE ASTRONOMER OF DUBLIN '
so that amongst loyal people of that town the
saying commonly runs—' God send to Dublin
many more such Astronomers ! '

The same conceit has some years back been
turned into rhyme by one Mr. Derrick, a gentleman formerly in the service of Sir Henry Sidney,
in whose poem we find it thus set forth—

> His head is poled high,
>   Upon the castle here,
> Beholding starres as though he were
>   A great Astronomier.

Of which poesy, [if poesy, good lack ! it must be
called ;] we may fairly methinks reverse the saying
and cry—'God send us no more such Poets ! '

though were the same singularity fitly treated, and by one who understood the management and composition of verses, it might, it seems to me, form a no unworthy theme for a loyal subject's muse.

This thought—I standing there, and looking up at it, though at this distance seemingly the head of a pin rather than of a man—I was moved to utter aloud, yet by some accident did not do so, and as it afterwards appeared fortunately, for about an hour later, we having in the meanwhile made the circuit of the city, and entered the Castle between the two gate towers, I lingered to look into the moat or fosse, which is here of great depth and blackness, being fed by a small but foul stream running along the Eastward side of the Castle. And looking down, and wondering greatly at its depth and opacity, I was told by Mistress Agatha that prisoners confined above in the towers did frequently endeavour to escape by dropping themselves into it, having first cut through, or otherwise got rid of their fetters. But it rarely, she said, happened that any escaped thereby, owing to the depth of the fosse, the foulness of the mud, and the slipperiness of the sides, so that after many toilsome efforts to escape

if none came to their aid, they for the most part
perished miserably.

'Marry, so better!' cried I merrily. 'Beshrew
me an' they like such a manner of death her
Majesty is the better contented, and her revenue
no doubt eased, not alone of the price of their food,
but also of a stout hempen cord, which would else
I take it be the natural end and shrift of all such
froward and ungrateful caitiffs!'

Having uttered these words, which I protest
I did in all simplicity, and without thought that
't were possible they could offend any hearer, I
chanced to turn my head in the direction of
Mistress Bridget, who stood a little to the left
of me. But when I did so I beheld her face
reddened with anger up to the very edge of her
coif, and her eyes like two fiery coals, darting
Death at me, I all unknowing what harm I had
done. And—

'Not content with slaying, must you needs gibe
and mock?' she began. Whereat the other damsel,
her companion, ran to her, whispering in her ear,
and endeavouring to smooth her down, as you may
see one ring-dove endeavour to smooth and comfort
another. But she would by no means listen, but
broke away, turning her head again towards me as

she went with eyes so full of wrath that I stood
all silent, amazed, and alarmed. And the next
moment she brake into torrents of weeping, such
as it pitied me to see, and thus angry, and thus
weeping, departed, hastening up a flight of steps,
leading I knew not whither, so that we speedily
lost sight of her.

Then the other damsel, [being left alone with
me, and seeing me still stand amazed and con-
fused], begged with many prayers that I would
reveal to no man what she was about to tell
me. Which I having strictly promised, she told
me that her cousin, having been bereft from in-
fancy of her parents, had in her early youth been
brought up by certain Burkes of the family of
Clanrickard, to which family her mother belonged,
and had moreover been betrothed when little past
childhood to a cousin of hers, one Felim Oge Burke,
a comely and gracious youth some few years older
than herself, who up to the beginning of the late
wars had dwelt, he and all his kinsfolk, in peace
and loyalty upon their own estates. When however the late great stir began the elder brother of
this youth's father fell away, and joined himself to
the Arch Rebel Tyrone. The younger brother
nevertheless still held aloof, in spite of which, he,

being come upon suddenly, was by the Lord
Deputy's orders seized and flung for greater
security into prison, which so enraged him that,
finding presently the means to escape, he brake
from his allegiance, and joined himself to his
brother and Tyrone, and, being afterwards again
taken prisoner, was duly executed, together with
some six or eight of his kinsfolk.   But this youth
—being so young, and having nothing found
against him—was by the graciousness of the Queen's
Majesty respited, and hath from that time unto the
present, being six years, lain in prison in Dublin
Castle, very grievously tormented with fetters, and
in evil case by reason of the foul air engendered by
those noisome vaults ; and sore complaineth of his
state, he having committed no sin, but suffering
solely because of the misdeeds of others.

' Truly,' said I, ' his is a piteous case, and if
opportunity serve I will not neglect to apprise my
Lord of it, so that haply some alleviation may
come to his state, and in due time with proper
precaution he may perchance be set at liberty.
Nevertheless, sweet Mistress Agatha, it is needless I
should expound to you, who art evidently a discreet
and a God-fearing maiden, that troubles oft over-
take men in this life, not merely by reason of their

own sin and frailty, but also by reason of the sin of those that went before them. For what saith the Second Commandment—" He shall visit the sins of the fathers upon the children even unto the third and fourth generation of them that hate him." What then is just and proper when done by an Heavenly Sovereign, must needs be just and right for an Earthly Sovereign to perform likewise.'

'Verily sir' said pretty Mistress Agatha. 'I am not wise enough nor learned enough in such matters to dispute with one who is my better, not merely in years but also in understanding. Nathe- less it seemeth to my poor reason that if the Queen's Majesty was but half ware of all that of this kind is done in her name in this realm of Ireland, she would give commandment to those that are set to execute her will and pleasure that they exercise a nicer discernment between those that are truly guilty, and deserving of chastisement, and they that by ignorance merely, or by the zeal of others are brought low, lest haply some, still at large, finding that such evil hap befalls those that are taken, should grow desperate, and choose rather to take part openly with the rebels than to submit, and fall into the like evil case.'

Hearing her speak thus prudently, I was silent

awhile, for in truth her words seemed to me full of reason, seeing how little even the wisest princes know of what goes on under their rule and sovereignty, but are themselves abused by those who for their own ends, and often from very wantonness, misuse their names.

Then Mistress Agatha, advancing, led the way before me up that flight of steps, onto a terrace which ran alongside of the Castle, being the same way by which her cousin Mistress Bridget had already gone. The sun was at that time shining brightly, a thing which as I had often heard, and ere long myself perceived, it seldom does in this Land of Ireland. The terrace was covered with grass growing tall and rank, showing that few passed there, but below there ran an under terrace leading to the bridge over the moat, which moat is, as I have already said, very deep, and running down to the bottom of the Castle vaults.

When we had ascended to the top we perceived Mistress Bridget standing a little way off looking down earnestly into this moat, her hands moving rapidly up and down as though she were speaking, yet was there no one near her.

Seeing this Mistress Agatha started, and made as if she would have gone back. Then, turning

to me, she again besought me very earnestly
not to betray her cousin, which I promising
readily not to do, she revealed to me that the
dungeon wherein was lodged that young Felim
Oge Burke of whom she had spoken, lay below
this terrace on which we walked, yet not so immediately below that he could descry one standing
thereon.   Nevertheless her cousin would from time
to time, she said, walk there, and, the weather being
fine and the sun shining behind her, her shadow
would be thrown upon the wall opposite, in such
manner that young Burke, looking from his dungeon window, could see and feast his eyes upon
this her image and distant presentment.   Which
tale, thus told, moved me greatly, as it seemed to
me that in all the tales of love I had ever heard
or read I had never met aught more moving or
more pitiful.

'Now by God's Grace!' cried I 'I were almost
content myself to suffer the like imprisonment
were I but assured that one would as willingly
mourn and wait for me as your cousin, fair Mistress Agatha, does for this young Burke!   Think
you, sweet maiden, were *your* troth plighted to
one that is no rebel, nor yet kin to rebels, but
a faithful, if humble subject of her Majesty, and

that some such evil hap befel him, would you also do as your cousin doth, namely mourn for him as truly, and wait for him as faithfully and as patiently ? '

'Nay sir,' said she casting down her eyes modestly, 'that were scarce needed, since such an one were little likely to come into the like evil case, seeing that he would be set in no such strait between his love and his duty as is the case with the poor youth who is betrothed to my cousin. Verily it is only in this sad distracted country that a man is so set betwixt his kindred and his obedience that t' were hard for him to know what to do or whom to follow, since whatever he doth that we may be sure will prove to be the very thing that for his own sake he were best have left undone.'

With that her eyes again overflowed piteously, seeing which my own could scarce forbear to keep them company, my heart seeming, as the Psalmist saith, even as wax in the midst of my body. And much I marvelled how the troubles of one who was after all but a Froward Rebel and doubtless a Papist to boot, should have so overcome me. Soon however I perceived that it was not his story, albeit a piteous one, but the manner and

look of sweet Mistress Agatha, and the fashion in
which she did tell of her cousin's grief. Indeed a
sweeter and fairer maiden I have never seen,
nor one whom a man might more joyfully take
to his breast. And I—who am, I confess, but a
very reed where her sweet sex is concerned—did
greatly long to wipe away those tears which,
though they dimmed her eyes, made them but
the fairer, as a pretty and odorous flower is but
the prettier and sweeter when it is overcast with
dew. And, my heart being thus full, I poured
out many words to comfort her ; which words I
do not now myself strictly recal, nor were it
seemly if I did that I should set them down
here, these pages being reserved for solider and
graver matters. Yet this I may say that many
words of sweet discourse passed between us
that morning, and that in all truth and hum-
bleness it seemed to me that the maiden was
herself not less well disposed for my company
and entertainment than I for a surety was for
hers.

For on the way back to Mr. Usher's house—
we having left Mistress Bridget to that sad exercise in which she took delight—my eyes seemed
continually drawn as it were by magnets to her

face, so that I could by no means detach them,
which, she perceiving, hung her head modestly,
yet not so completely down but what from time
to time I caught sight of her blushing visage,
nay more than once was favoured with a very
soft and kindly glance from her eyes, which like
the dart of Venus' Son so fired and enflamed my
breast that I grew deeply enamoured of her
tender perfections, and could scarce forbear in
words to declare my passion.   And, thus sucking
in the Honey of Love, I walked along, rather as
if on air, or the soft clouds of Heaven, than upon
the miry ways of this foul city of Dublin.

   ' Oh thou strange and mysterious Divinity of
Love ! ' said I to myself as I so journeyed.   ' Of
what an unaccountable and ficklesome nature
art thou, ever delighting to shoot thine arrows at a
venture, so that a man may depart from his house
in the morning whole and unwounded, and return
to it within the space of an hour so pricked, sore,
and desperate that he can no longer call his heart
his own ! '

   Yet, lest any think from these my inward
utterances and interjections that so speedy a
love must needs rest upon unstable foundation,
this will I say in my own behoof [though little

given to the folly of self-justification,] that I was never one of those hasty lovers whose suit all endeth in a few quick sighs, nor yet of those who like ramage kites see in each new Fair a prey, but have ever set my heart with a loyal and faithful service upon her whom I loved. For which reason perchance it is that it has been my lot to find trouble where I looked for solace, and grief when I most expected joy, a thing which has bred in me a sort of settled Melancholy, or despondent Humour, so that scarce do I look for ought now but sorrow and disappointment.

Still Hope is a sweet string even in the saddest lute, and therefore I, whose love-sorrows have been far greater than common—[as is known and admitted by all who have been witnesses of the same]—do nevertheless cherish a hope of better things, and take Fortune's buffets with such patience as I may, hoping that having long whipped me with scorpions, she may at last perchance salve me with roses. Yet what is this life of ours at best but a Vale of Disappointment, so that in this world it is not a man's deserts, nor yet the extremity of his patience that will give him the recompense, else had we never seen some whom I could name exalted

D

far above their merits, while others who by modesty and patience have deserved her favours, the cruel jade Fortune pays out with slights, and injuries. Yet that in so doing she but enableth them to prove the greatness, and tenacity of their love is to be admitted.   For as hath been well said in a pleasant-conceited volume late writ and given to the world—'As the moon is never seen without the star Lunesiqua, so a true and faithful lover was never known to be without Unrest.'

III

BEING early returned to the house and his Excellency having still no need of my services and my heart being so full of Mistress Agatha, tied as it seemed with knots to her tender perfections, I hastily took pen and tablet, and sat down to indite a sonnet ; an habit which has ever been a solace to me, as to other lovers, alike whether their stars be kind or cruel, though not one to be indulged in beyond the limits of a due discretion. And this sonnet began thus,—

> Oh strange-hued love ! great Nature's joy and ban !
> Thou wound, yet unguent of this dolorous earth !
> Thou sweetest torment of sad-hearted man !
> Thou gentle savage ! thou distressful mirth !
> Here all forlorn I sit me down and sing
> Thy piercing darts, so cruel and so sweet ;
> Whose tender sting such honeyed sorrows bring,
> Whose bitter joys . . . .

Now I had just reached the middle of this line, and was even debating in my mind what should be a fitting rhyme to the preceding one,

when I heard the voice of young Frank Gardner
raised without, and another voice with his, seeming
to dispute with him, and both coming closer and
closer.   Dropping my pen, therefore, I ran to the
door, but hardly had I reached it before I was met
and all but overturned by him and another young
lad of his own age, who were coming along, and
disputing lustily one with the other.

' How now Frank ? How now ? ' cried I, so soon
as I had regained my balance.   'Do you take
yourself to be in one of your West Country taverns
where you may brawl your fill, or of what think
you to let your voice be heard in this unseemly
fashion in my lord's very antechamber ?   Nay
shame gentlemen ! shame ! shame !   What means
this insolence ?   Down with your hands both of
you ! '

For he and the other youngster were squaring
up to one another, and both had their hands on
their swords, as if about to draw, and their
faces red with anger ; only that Frank's eyes were
wide open, like two turquoise stones in a ring,
whereas the other, whose eyes were dark and
narrow in shape, had them ·cast down, and an ugly
look upon his face, which was of a sallow, ·spotty,
and unwholesome aspect.

'Beshrew thee, Hal, hold thy tongue, and meddle not in my matters!' cried Frank, turning upon me, hot and angry as a turkey cock. 'How shouldst thou judge between us, seeing that thou knowest not what this villain hath said? For when I spoke of my Lord having come to Ireland to chastise all traitors, and especially the Arch-traitor Tyrone who stands at defiance against her Majesty he scoffed! I tell you he scoffed at me! and declared that my Lord would never dare face Tyrone, no nor any Lord that the Queen could send, for that since the late defeat of the Black-water the fame of Tyrone has waxed so great that no man durst meet him in the field, aye and that the very Queen herself and they that be of her Council have fear of him!'

'Nay I said not so' answered the other 'I said that none had as yet done so, and more-over——'

With that Frank broke in again—'But I say thou didst!' he roared. 'And will prove the same upon thy body! yea and think myself little honoured to fight one of so poor and dastardly a spirit! And as for this Tyrone of whom thou pratest, I would meet him myself tomorrow with any weapons he might choose, either on foot or horse-back! Meet him! aye would eat him alive, and without salt too, rather than it should go abroad that none of English breeding durst affront him!'

' Come, come ; enough of all this Frank!' said I ' this place is not made for such loud swash-buckler language and bearing. And for you, young sir, whose countenance I know not,' con-tinued I turning to the other, ' 'twere better me-thinks you retired, and 'twere not ill perchance that you reflected too upon how little such a fashion of regarding the Queen's service is be-coming to that uniform which I see you wear, or to the duty of an officer and man of quality ; which duty is as is well known to foster the spirit and daring of his men, who by their baser birth are by nature less attuned to nobleness, and not to balk or discourage them by uttering ought that could cast doubt upon the sure victory of her Majesty's forces, still less to the vaunting of those vile traitors who have already grown only too strong through the weakness of those that opposed them.'

Then the youngster (who was as I afterwards learnt a cornet newly entered into the company of Sir Henry Harrington) bowed to me and departed, not sorry I took it to escape without further assault from so doughty an antagonist. But Frank could I with difficulty restrain, so hot was he with wrath, and so burning to reek the same upon all who should gainsay him. And, forcing him to remain with me, he raged to and fro the room, declaring that all whom he had as yet met in this country [save those who had come over in our own company] were little better themselves than rebels and traitors, and that their craven talk was enough to make a brave man blush, and that for his part he would gladly fight them all, aye every cowardly Man-Jack of them, ere ever he advanced to the encounter of Tyrone, and the larger traitors.

So—having listened to him awhile and getting weary of his talk, and being wishful to return to my former recreation—I was forced at last to chide him in earnest, telling him that such language was unbecoming the modesty due from one that was himself but a beardless lad, and had never yet seen swords crossed in angry war ; adding that he reminded me most of some child that, having been set by its Grandam a-cock-horse upon a Painted Stick, holds itself henceforward to be a full grown man and a warrior.

At which saying of mine—though I meant it in

Davidson College Library

all kindness—he grew only the more furious, and burst away, nor would any longer be restrained ; being ever, I grieve to say, of a hot and choleric temper, and not a little spoiled by his mother, who poor soul, (he being her only child, and fatherless from his birth), could never sufficiently love or make much of him. Yet this will I admit, though oft vexed by his unreasonable behaviour, that I have never known a lad whose soul was freer from that base sediment which, choking the free channels of youth, causeth it often to become muddy, nor one that showed a more generous and gallant spirit, so that few ever came to know him without speedily learning to love and cherish him above the common.

But touching Tyrone—which this quarrel betwixt Frank and the other youngster brings before me—this seems a good place to let the reader understand (as none who have not been in Ireland could in truth believe and know) that the fame of that vile Arch-rebel and Capital traitor has so gone abroad in this kingdom that all men tremble at the very bruiting thereof. For beginning in Ulster, his main strength and the seat of his power, it hath spread into Connaught, (where the Burkes and other chiefs there are his close allies and abettors), thence to Munster, and afterward to Leinster, where all but the towns of Dublin, Kilkenny, and some few of the chief places of the Pale have fallen into his hands, the cattle too, which are the chief wealth of the country, being all in his possession, so that any force sent against him is like to starve. And this state of things has not come about suddenly, but has grown and strengthened for the space of two years past, being fed by the weakness of those that should have opposed it, and especially by that great and lamentable overthrow of Sir Richard Bagnal the Marshall at the ford of the Blackwater ; where, (the two forces being equal or nearly so) the Queen's troops were miserably put to flight with great loss, shame, and discouragement, and the greater encouragement of those who take part in these foul and monstrous treasons.

That I have formerly heard my Lord maintain that this Tyrone was less absolutely blameworthy in the first instance than did appear I must admit, he having, it seems, in past years served her Majesty well as a soldier, both in Munster under the Lord Grey, and in his own province of Ulster, and would, my Lord held, have continued to do so but for the hindrances of those sent from England to bear rule in that province. In so saying however he judged that Traitor rather I believe by his own noble nature than by ought that appertaineth to the same, he being (so far as ever I could learn) brim-full of insolence and ungodly cunning, so that if his mind was ever set upon the paths of loyalty it has long since utterly departed therefrom.

But touching our present expedition, which chiefly concerns these pages, it was without doubt her Majesty's intention that so soon as my Lord should arrive he should proceed direct to the North, there to encounter this Arch Traitor and his following, so that he might quickly be taught obedience, and his proud stomach reduced to lowliness and humility. That such had been also his Lordship's own intention I who know his thoughts can by no means hesitate to declare. Yet occasion will arise which obligeth even the fullest and clearest purposes to be laid aside ; as will be admitted by all save those so assured in their own conceits that they make nothing of such hindrances as even God himself sets, and to which the greatest must bow. For when his Lordship was come to Dublin he found the new levies there gathered to be so poor, weak, and ill equipped as to be scarce worthy of the name of soldiers, having, as he himself said, 'neither bodies, spirits, nor practice of arms.' This being the case it seemed more agreeable to sound policy first to .visit the weaker rebels, and, assuring the south and west frontiers of the Pale by sufficient garrisons, to raze those strong places in Munster and Connaught which have so long resisted the Queen's officers, and, having thus tested the strength of the army against what was less difficult and arduous, afterwards to proceed to that which was harder and more hazardous.

That this opinion was held, not alone by his Excellency, but also by all that under him bear rule in Ireland is clear, seeing that the letter to her Majesty and the English Privy Council was signed by the whole Irish Council, to wit, amongst others —Thomas, Lord Bishop of Meathe, Sir George Carew, Sir Nicholas Walshe, Sir Conyers Clifford the President of Connaught, Sir Henry Harrington, Sir Warham St. Leger, Sir Geoffrey Fenton and others. Nay, not merely did they counsel it, but earnestly pressed it upon him, advising him—' that it was expedient for her Majesty's service that the invasion of Ulster should be for a time respited, and a present prosecution put on first in Leinster, that province being ever the heart and centre of this Kingdom.

Words, however, [especially such weak and impotent words, as I may hope to utter] are I know of little avail in the face of such loud-winded bugges, and foul lies as have been set abroad in this matter ; so that even those who know best to the contrary shame not to utter them, declaring that through slackness it was on my Lord's part that Tyrone was not sooner met and overcome. Whereas all who have seen him can declare how he hath laboured day and night, not sparing himself, even when sore wasted by illness, but being ever at work upon the Queen's service. A thing the more readily proved but that like some noble eagle he is one that pursueth his own way heedless of the clamour of meaner creatures, until, becoming all at once aware of their malice, he turns upon them with beak and claws ; thereby unhappily often in his anger rather aiding their slanders than establishing his own right and innocency.

For this since ever I knew him I have remarked in my Lord of Essex, that whereas other men injure themselves by their faults, he rather by his virtues, and by that noble boldness of his nature which can by no means be concealed. For so frank is he by constitution that even in the presence of the Queen's Majesty he will utter

nought but what he holds to be the very Truth of
Truths, opening his soul before her with a freedom
seldom to be heard of Sovereigns, more especially
one ever accounted a Goddess, rather than a Queen
or Woman, and little fitted therefore to brook
opposition, even where the necessities of State
require the same. Who, being at the present
time somewhat enfeebled in health, suffereth con-
tradiction the less patiently, though none the less
now as throughout her reign endowed with every
great and glorious quality, in which she so far
exceedeth in splendour not only every Monarch
that at the present time breathes upon the Globe, but
also all who in the most distant pages of History
have ever been seen, known, or heard of!

IV

FOR the rest of our stay in Dublin, little methinks
remains to be recorded, the chief event of the time
being that great disturbance caused by the dis-
placement of my Lord Southampton, who had on
his arrival been appointed by the Lord Lieutenant
General of the Horse in Ireland, which appoint-
ment their LL's the Lords of the Council did at
her Majesty's order command to be cancelled ; a
command which his Excellency at first refused to
obey, declaring that her Majesty had in his com-
mission given him full liberty to make choice
of all such officers and commanders of the army
as he thought fitting. This their LL's could by
no means deny, nevertheless, [her Majesty being so
fully determined, and my lord Southampton by
reason of his late marriage in sore disfavour] his
Excellency in the end was constrained to obey ;
which he did very unwillingly, declaring that
such changes in the face of the enemy but

encouraged the rebels, and dismayed the army, of which too large a portion was already disposed to look upon this expedition as but a cold and comfortless action.

Touching mine own poor matters—which have no right, I know, to find place in a record given to those of larger and more weighty import —this may I say that it was my happiness to hold sundry further discourses with fair Mistress Agatha Usher, which discourses were both pleasant at the time and joyful to remember ; and that upon my departure I prayed her acceptance of a small Casket of Poesy, or Modest Handful of Dainty Delights, a request which she graciously complied with, promising to read therein, and now and then as I prayed her to reflect upon their poor Author. And this promise she made, looking so modest and withal loving, that I rode away, poor Fool, my heart overflowing like some great river, and my spirit stirred to martial deeds like a very Paladin. A mood which I must honestly say is not with me habitual, I being rather given to the ways of peace than of war, though through my service to his Lordship often finding myself amid the clash of swords, on which occasion I have never failed to acquit myself so as to win

no little commendation from all that were witnesses of the same.

The fourth day of May being come and the
levies gathered together, the Lord Lieutenant
rode forth from Dublin to the champion fields
between Kilrush and Kilcullen, where he had
appointed to meet him twenty seven ensigns of
foot and three hundred horse, which he proposed
to divide into regiments, appointing colonels for
the same. These troops being already assembled
upon the field, so soon as they saw his Excellency
riding up, raised a great shout, so that the very sky
seemed filled with the noise, and all drew their
swords and waved them, shouting together with
one voice—'God save Ireland's Governor!' 'God
preserve the noble Earl of Essex!'

At which sound, and the tumult it bred,
young Frank Gardner, [who that day rode beside
me, and could scarce even before be contained,
so great was his joy to find himself at length in
truth a soldier, and in the field], suddenly snapped
his sword out of its scabbard, and waved it
thrice over his head, shouting lustily the while.
And this shouting, continuing after the others had
ceased and his voice being so young and fresh, and
coming from our own side, was heard throughout

the entire army, so that his Excellency himself
turned round, and laughed to see the boy so proud.
Whom I would have silenced, being surprised
that he should thus demean himself without license
given, but his Lordship commanded me to forbear,
swearing that the lad was after his own heart, and
that he would he had Ten Thousand of him, so
that he might the more readily bring those rebels
to submission which sinned against her Majesty's
patience, and troubled the peace of the Realm.

These champion fields are called by the natives
'Curaghs' and are of a very singular size and flatness, the grass which covereth them short but
of a close consistency. A better place for the de-
ploying of an army I never beheld, nor could I
forbear to wish that the Arch Rebel Tyrone and
all the other enemies of the Queen's Highness
would but encounter us here in their strength, so
that we might the better make an end of them.

That night, there being no town nearer than
the Naas, we were forced to lie in a village called
Kilcullen, a sorry cluster of mean houses, and they
so few that he who had a roof to lie under was
accounted happy. Young Frank Gardner, and
myself lay together in a small hut or cabin which
had been assigned to Sir Conyers Clifford, the

E

President of Connaught, who courteously proffered us a share of his quarters; which truth to tell were neither commodious nor savoury, indeed so foul a hut I never thought to set foot or nose in.

It being the first night of taking to the field since our coming to Ireland the confusion was great; there being as yet no tents, so that they that could not find shelter under a roof, must needs sleep under the open sky. In every direction there were squires searching for their masters; great Lords not knowing where to lay their heads; horses fastened with stanchions to the earth; cloaks of great price flung heedless upon the foul and muddy ground.

This village of Kilcullen lies upon either side of a bridge of planks which crosses the river Liffey, the same which passeth through Dublin, and which here winds with wondrous sudden twists and turns. In number it contains perhaps twenty cabins, the owners of which had fled leaving them empty [saving for certain inmates whose company might well have been spared !]. Fitter place for the harbouring of pigs, and less fit for the quarters of a great Earl and General in Chief of her Majesty's forces 'twere difficult in truth to imagine.

My Lord's own quarters were in the principal house in the village, which, being two stories high, was doubtless of these savages accounted a palace. When I went in to him he was sitting upon a great heap of straw gathered together in the middle of the room, with a light fixed above his head, and a letter newly writ upon his knee.

'Well Signor Pegaso!' quoth he, laying down his pen as I entered. 'And what thinkest thou of these quarters of ours? Didst ever see loftier or prouder roof than yonder?' pointing over his head to where the sorry thatch was broken, so that through it one could descry the sky, and a faint twinkling of stars which had now begun to shine in the midst thereof.

'Truly my Lord' said I ''tis a rueful sight, and 'twould pity her Majesty's heart methinks could she see you as I do at this moment'

'Not so Hal, I thought you knew her Grace's mind better. For what wrote she to my father when he laboured in this Irish service even as I do now 'T'were better' quoth she 'to desire to live in action, rather than to fester in the delights of this English Egypt, where the most part of those bred in the soil find their chief joy in holding their noses over the beef pots!'

'For beef pots my Lord,' said I ruefully 'there be none here that I can see, and for my part I were not sorry, I own, we were more like to enjoy the savour of the same.'

'Ho! ho! soft and sweet, great Son of the Muses!' cried he laughingly. 'Has that poetic soul of thine sunk to this pass already? Nay man take courage, and buckle in thy stomach belt a bit tighter, lest the divine Afflatus inside escape thee altogether for lack of sustenance!'

Then, (seeing that I looked abashed, and had no response ready, jesting speech being apt I own to find in me a lagging playfellow) he enquired more seriously how I fared in this disordered camp, where few had aught to lie on or to eat. Whereupon I told him of the kindness showed us by the President of Munster, how he had offered myself and young Frank Gardner a share of his quarters, whereby we should have at least some roof atop of us (albeit a poor one) and not have to couch like swine upon the filthy earth.

''Twas well thought of' replied his Excellency, 'and I am glad that thou and that wild lad of thine have found shelter, since 'tis hard on an unseasoned youth to begin his soldiering upon sore bones. Touching Sir Conyers too, his goodwill is the plainer you-wards, seeing that he does it not to gain favour in my sight, I having for a good time past held him to belong rather to the faction of mine enemies than mine own.'

'There I am sure' cried I 'you wrong him my Lord!'

'Say you so Hal? May be, and in truth I find myself so bound about with lies and liars, that an honest man, were he ten thousand times my enemy, were better to me than one of yonder crook-tongued, court-infesting knaves. By the Thunders of God! I know not how a plain man keeps his hands off them! I tell you, Hal, my gorge rises at the bare thought of them, even as at the thought of so many toads and adders. Nay more, for those beasts but spread their slime according to the nature God gave them, whereas these others out of sheer evil heartedness, trying how to entrap those that be fairer and of more open nature than themselves.'

So saying his Excellency began to pace the room to and fro with a disordered countenance, showing me plainly that some new cause of displeasure were stirring within him. Finding that he spake not again I presently enquired whether he had any commands to give me, or if there was ought I should write at his dictation. To which he replied that he had but to finish one letter newly writ to her Grace, which must be needs be done with his own hand, and that for the rest tomorrow would suffice.

With that, smoothing his countenance somewhat, he took up again the letter which lay beside him. And as he passed his eyes over it, presently his lips began to twitch, as if some sudden conceit was stirring within him. And——

'By Nemesis!' cried he, slapping down upon the paper with his hand, 'I talk, but I am of the same Sorry Crew myself! I tell thee, Hal, I scarce know myself sometimes when I read what honeyed words seem to have slid along my paper. Assuredly Francis was right when he told me that my pen was a safer ambassador to her Grace's favour than my tongue. For I can spin as courtier-like a letter as any of yonder rascals that juggle with words, but when it comes to open speech—God's mercy upon me!—either my temper or my honesty leaps abroad, and the Devil is in it if I know which of the two is most out of place at court, or most like to bring a man to trouble there.'

' Others can give your Lordship prudent advice as well as Master Bacon,' said I.

' Meaning thyself, most discreet of counsellors ? ' Nay, be not jealous, good Wisdom ! be not jealous ! Believe me I apprise your fidelity at its full value. And for other matters one would not sure have all ones councillors cut out upon the one pattern, and a second Francis—if indeed two Francis Bacons are to be found in any universe—would I confess be the death, end, and undoing of any man's faith in his fellows, which for my part I desire not ; for though Suspicion, I admit, is a wise dog, yet Trust, as I have before told him, I believe at bottom to be a better one.'

' Methinks such suspiciousness comes of looking too closely into his own heart, my Lord ' said I. For in truth this Master Bacon is no favourite of mine, nor, as I judge, always the soundest of councillors to his Excellency.

' Of looking too closely into the heart—if heart is the word—of that foul Creep-thing a courtier, Hal, who, as Francis hath himself said, would crook all things to his private ends, and willingly any day set fire to a house so long as he could thereby roast his own eggs at it. But no more o' them ! Their very name corrupts the atmosphere,

which in this close and dung-bestrewn cabin is, by
my Faith, none too savoury already. Meanwhile, go
thy ways, good fellow, go thy ways, and betake thee
to rest, if rest is to be had. And hark, a word in
thy ear! Tell the President of Connaught I
would fain have some private speech with him, and
that I beg him therefore to come to me here ere
we set out in the morning, that being like to be
the surest and least observed time.'

To this I replied that I would do so, and,
having made my bow, I departed, thrice missing
my way between his Lordship's lodging and the one
which I was in search of, and getting all befouled
with the filthy mire, which in many places was knee
deep and over.

But when I at last reached the cabin where
I was to sleep I found a great case or box had
been dragged into the midst of it, and on it
were set forth sundry bottles, likewise a goodly
round of beef, and capon pie; a sight which
I own caused my heart to leap up gladly within
my body, I having greatly feared to go to bed
wholly supperless that night.

And at the head of this box now conformed
into a table sat good Sir Conyers Clifford, with
his helmet, which he had worn all day, laid aside,

showing a great scar running across from the forehead nearly to the chin, by which his face was
much disfigured, yet not so badly but what it
was as goodly and soldierly a one as I desire
to look on, albeit so rugged and wrinkled. And
on the left hand of him sat young Frank Gardner, with his helmet doffed too, and his blue eyes
all of a dance, and his face still smooth as a
maiden's in May, and in his hand a great clasp
knife, which he was plunging deep into the bowels
of that pasty. And with them sat two other
gentlemen, one of whom was unknown to me,
the other being a cousin of Sir Conyers, by
name also Clifford, who served under him as his
equerry.

But when Frank Gardner espied me at the
door he set up a great shout of welcome, as
though he and none other were Lord of that
good cheer, and desired that I would straightway
enter in, and sit and eat of all that was going.

'How now; how now Master Malapert?' said
I rebukingly, 'knowest thou no better, nor canst
do greater credit to thy breeding than to roar
out thus like a young bullock in a clover field?
Nay the Lord President of Connaught is far too
good to thy unhandsome deserts. 'Twere fitter

thou wert sent to sup with his horseboys, till thou learnest respect for those that are set over thee by Nature and Providence !'

'Pooh, pooh ; chide not the lad' said good Sir Conyers kindly. 'In truth it pleasures me to see one to whom life has still a goodly savour in the mouth, and for whom a journey like this, to most of us but a burdensome and little honourable enterprise, is an occasion for rejoicing. Marry he will learn but too soon to find the briars and thorns that grow on every bush, so let him pluck the roses while he may! Meanwhile prithee approach, good Mr. Secretary, and help yourself to what there is, which to tell truth is more than I expected to find, seeing that everything is still in such confusion and disorder.'

At that I approached to the board, giving him many thanks, and sat down gladly on a great heap of hay, gathered for the foraging of the horses. Under our feet was nought but the puddled mud of the cabin, such as these savage creatures use to sit on, and the roof overhead so low and so rotten that any rain dropping through would speedily have wet and soddened all below.

But Frank,—little daunted by my rebukes which he ever heeded only too little—was like one that had already drunk his fill, so glad was he, and his tongue babbling continually, like the tongue of some young sea-pye late escaped the nest. And amongst other weighty matters he told me that Sir Henry Harrington, by whose side it seems he had ridden that afternoon, had offered him a cornetcy in his company, and that he was hugely minded to accept the same, expecting to see more service, and to get a larger share of fighting than he otherwise might.

' Nay, Frank, softly, softly ; we will talk of this anon,' said I. For in truth I liked not that Sir Henry Harrington over much, and had heard but ill things of the courage and discipline of his soldiers ; also I desired to keep Frank under my own eye, having been so largely the occasion of his coming to this country, and having many fears lest his rashness and inexperience should bring him to speedy danger.

Then, the solidest part of the viands being all eaten, we set ourselves to dispose of the wine, which was both abundant and choice. But before doing so, Sir Conyers, rising with a full cup in his hand, called out in a loud voice—' Success to the Earl of Essex, and God confound the Queen's enemies !' which toast being drunk by us with

loud acclaim—Frank Gardner's voice needless to
say loudest of all—there came running in to us
three or four gentlemen from my Lord of Southampton's lodging, which was hard by ; and they,
finding how matters were, stayed also, and so by
degrees others gathered, till there was a good score
or more in the room, and a strange sight it was
to see so many fine cloaks and gallant gentlemen
and goodly weapons pent in that foul hut, which
till that day had never, I ween, seen ought but the
stabling of pigs, or of such as in point of breeding
differed little from the same.

One of these gentlemen, Captain Hubert
Blackett by name, a captain of an hundred under
Sir Alexander Ratcliffe, being endowed with a
good singing voice, and some knowledge of har-
mony, was persuaded after some little entreaty
to sing to the company. And afterwards another
gentleman and another did the same. Then Sir
Conyers—having heard that I belonged myself to
the Rhymer's craft—would have it I must favour
the company with some taste of my quality ; which
proposal I would have declined, not alone from
modesty, but from having nought in my wallet that
seemed suitable to the occasion, or to so mixed
a company.

Despite of all I could say, however, he would take no denial, and they that were sitting there also importuned me, especially Captain Blackett; saying that when one had played or sung it was the duty of the rest to do their part. So, being over-persuaded, I rehearsed certain lines that I had recently composed since my thoughts had been running upon fair Mistress Usher. Which lines I here set down, praying the reader to understand that their poor quality must not be taken as a sample of what I may or in past times have done of the same sort.

Like to a plot of fairest garden ground,
Where all compacted sweets united lie,
Is She whose image my sad soul doth bound
With thought and love of her eternally.
And every mile but adds a lengthening chain
To that soft gyve which causes all my pain.

Shall roving Phœbus ope his wanton eye
On the pure heavens of her most tender face?
While I alas! in weary exile lie
And banished far from hope of love and grace?
And every mile but adds a lengthening chain
To that soft gyve which causeth all my pain.

This woeful land wherein I sadly stray
Is not so sad as my fond heart and true,
Far from that Lady whose soft grace I pray,
To whose deserts my hourly vows are due.
And every mile but adds a lengthening chain
To that sad gyve which causes all my pain.

*　　*　　*　　*　　*　　*

Now there were about ten verses more, but, ere I had concluded this last one, and while the words were still in my mouth, Frank Gardner, who all that day had been excited above his wont, sprang from his seat, and striking lustily with his hand upon the board, so that all thereon rattled, cried to me in a loud voice that my song was of too sable a hue for the time and place, and did rather dispirit the hearts of those that sat there, than add to their merriment, or encourage them to valiant deeds.

' Marry ' quoth he ' I had as lief be a monk and drone pater-nosters as utter my soul with the like dolorous ditties! Women are fair, and I their humble servant, yet a *Man* is a *Man*, and it were a poor tribute to his manhood if all his thoughts must needs run upon what he has left behind him, so that he can spare none for that which lies before, and on which his manhood chiefly depends! By the sword and helmet of Mars! no such puling love for me!

With that he began to troll out some verses he had picked up, Heaven knows where, which in truth were of little credit either to him or their maker, and which as far as I remember ran thus—

By all the loves and all the doves
And all the sighs that lovers sigh !
By all the arts and all the darts
Of Cupid's feathered panoply !
Not every Fair that walks the earth
Nor every Goddess in the sky
Should keep *my* soul in Love's confines
When I might hope to do or die !
When I could go
To the wars, Heigho !
With my helmet laced,
And my breast-plate braced,
And my good sword strapped to my side, Heigho !

Shall Love's alarms deter the brave
His arrows set him flying Oh !
Shall fetters make his soul a slave
And set his breast a sighing Oh !
No, not though Cupid's fiery dart
Shone fierce in every Fair One's eye,
Would *I* forswear the soldier's part
Where I might hope to do or die !
When I could go
To the wars, Heigho !
With my helmet laced,
And my breast-plate braced,
And my good sword strapped to my side, Heigho !

Not all the sighs or all the tears
That women's beaming looks inspire !
Not all the hopes or all the fears
That set men's hearts and breasts a fire !
Shall keep *my* soul in Love's confines
When I may hope to do or die !
When I can go
To the wars, Heigho !
With my helmet laced,
And my breast-plate braced,
And my good sword strapped to my side, Heigho !

Which song, thus sung, and the round face and soft beardless cheek of the singer, who boasted himself so loudly to be a *Man*, set all the company a laughing. Nay I myself could scarce forbear to join, albeit not a little displeased to be so openly mocked of him before them all. And in my mind I privily resolved to give Master Frank a sharp and wholesome reprimand upon the very first occasion I found myself alone with him. And (the evening now growing late) after a few more sallies of merriment the company dispersed ; the gentlemen gathering up their swords and cloaks, and departing to their own quarters ; we seeking what repose so poor and damp a sleeping place might be looked to furnish.

V

NEXT day the army advanced towards Athy, which is upon the river Barrow, over a flat country, much desolated by the tribes of the O'Byrnes, O'Moores, and other fierce and pestilent rebels. And I, being newly come to Ireland, looked round me in terror of heart at the waste and desolations through which we passed; though afterwards, by comparison with what I saw later, I then esteemed this part prosperous and well liking.

His Excellency was riding in front of the army, with the Earl of Southampton on the one hand and Sir Conyers Clifford on the other, with whom that day I observed that he held much discourse. I was myself about a company and a half behind, and, as those in front halted to allow the rear guard to come up, I too stood aside to watch the army as it deployed through the narrow space. A gallant sight and goodly it was to see so many well armed men and fair steeds; the footmen too,

F

carrying their pikes and halberds. Yet methought there was little of that Joyousness which should illumine a soldier's countenance when he goes to meet the foe; nay, many of the faces on which my eyes rested wore a lowering and malcontent air, as though their owners' minds turned to other thoughts than their joy as a soldier and their duty to the Queen's Majesty.

There happened to be riding beside me on that occasion one Colonel Sethcock, a gentleman of some 45 or 50 years of age, who had come over to Ireland during the Desmond wars, and had since remained here, attached for the most part to the train of the Earl of Ormonde; whom I had never seen before, and in truth liked not greatly, though it was said that he had done good service. For his talk ran on the slaughter that in former wars had been wrought amongst the rebels; not so much upon those taken in arms (against whom no severities could be too great) but upon those that resisted not, but were nevertheless slain, though demanding their lives with earnest prayers and supplications; and of the women too and children of rebels, that were taken as hostages; the latter being for the most part too ignorant by reason of their tender age to judge between right or wrong, yet were nevertheless slain, sometimes even with torture, for the greater punishments of their parents. So that I grew vexed at such talk, which seemed to me unbefitting a soldier; being not of doughty deeds, but of such acts as a man, even if constrained to permit, doth so reluctantly, and in no wise glorieth to look back upon. And, for my part, I was sure, I said, that my Lord would never give ear to such counsel, nor permit of such doings, which seemed in my poor opinion to savour rather of savages than of soldiers and Christian gentlemen.

At which saying of mine Colonel Sethcock laughed loudly, smiting his thigh the while.

' Nay' cried he, ' if his Lordship is of so pitiful a temper he will scarce do for Ireland, where mildness is of as much use as tender handling avails for the throttling of savage beasts.'

' Even savage beasts,' I replied, ' are tamed, not by those that are savage like themselves, but by those who, being better than they, have become their masters, and so subdue them to their uses.'

' You will sing a different song Master Secretary when you have been here a little longer !' quoth he.

And then, for very despite as I thought at my words, he went on to tell other tales, which exceeded all ever I heard, and especially of one

village—the name of which at present escapes me
—where he, being present, he said, with a goodly
company of soldiers, did drive all that were therein,
men, women, and children, into a bog ; and this bog
being of great deepness, and they prevented by the
soldiers from escaping, they all perished miserably.

Which deed, [though done I admit against
rebels], fairly turned my stomach, so that I moved
away, and would no longer keep company with
him, but consorted afterwards that day chiefly
with Captain Charles Warren, brother of Sir
William Warren, and accounted at that time the
handsomest man in the Irish army ; who though
barely 30 years of age had for his services received
early promotion, and already commanded many
that for age and length of service stood higher
than himself.

To him I opened my mind, being still full of
these matters, and knowing him to be discreet, and
to have already acquired a sound knowledge of the
things that pertain to this land ; which of all lands
that ever I heard of seems the one most difficult
for a stranger to understand, and in which all
rules elsewhere laid down for a man's guidance
seem to be as it were reversed and made invalid.

'It is of a certainty a hard country, as you

truly say, Master Secretary,' said he. 'And this
I will tell you that when first I came to it my
stomach often turned, even as yours doth, at the
very name of things which at last grew to be
little accounted by me, save as matters of daily
occurrence. Nay, in the first expedition I was
engaged in against the rebels in Ulster, the cries of
those we slew, and of the women especially, rang in
my ears, so that I could get no sleep for thinking
of them. And oftentimes I would say to myself
" What fashion is this to treat men, who, if they are
savages and rebels, are still of flesh and blood
like ourselves, created in the self-same image of
Almighty God ? And if they are papists, marry,
why so were our own fathers or grandfathers, so
that seems scarce sufficient reason for treating
them like beasts, without souls or natural feeling."
Little by little however it came to be clear to me
that there was but one way of dealing with this
country, and that was to slay without ruth or
remorse, so that, if for no other reason, the very
terror and expectation of the like treatment might
keep the rest from rebelling. And this I may
tell you, Master Secretary, and it is, (if you forgive my saying so, being I believe somewhat your
junior) a lesson you were wise to lay to your

heart, namely that when a man's duty bids him
do a thing, were he the tenderest soul that
ever wept at sight of another's wounds, he must
learn to stomach it, and say naught ; so that by
degrees, the habit coming with practice, he will
learn to see unmoved things which at first sight
made his very soul to heave and sicken, and his
hand to fly to the sword for the avenging thereof.
For see you not how many things in life must
needs be done, and resolutely done, which in
themselves seem cruel and piteous.   Yea even the
very slaughter of sheep and oxen, and the wringing
of the necks of pullets, turn some tender stomachs.
Consider too the cutting off of arms and legs, and
the cauterizing of wounds with red hot irons, which
must be done to save life.   How think you the
surgeons would ever learn their trade if their hearts
were so tender that at the first loud cry they gave
way ?   Then take you again executions, which
are part of the duty of a state, necessary for the
punishment of malefactors, and under the special
sanction of Holy Writ, how often they seem
to the natural man cruel and unnecessary ?   I
remember not long since I was coming past the
place of execution at Devizes, very early in the
morning, and they were executing an old woman

who had stolen six penny-worth of bread, and
I who speak to you Master Secretary may confess that when I saw her struggling to escape,
and two men holding her, and her grey hair all
disordered, and her face contorted with the pangs
and terror of death, it was as much as I could do
to hinder myself from going to her aid ; for after all
she was a woman and an old one, and there was
something about her, too, which minded me, I
know not why, of my mother, for whose sake all old
women are dear to me, save such as do practise
Witchcraft, and are for that reason properly and
naturally abhorred both of God and man. So too
mutilation, and the racking or other torturing of
criminals that refuse to confess to crimes committed
by themselves or others. What can be more displeasing to the natural man ? Nevertheless those
learned in jurisprudence hold that the latter is a
thing necessary to be retained, to be used of course
with due discretion, and never without the sanction
of some civil officer, but as a mode of extorting
confession an indispensable handmaiden and as-
sistant of the Law. From which digression return
we to this question of Ireland, and to the means by
which it is to be brought into subjection. And with
regard to that severity, which like yourself I am at

times disposed to deplore, I tell you plainly that since coming to know the country, and especially since hearing the talk of those whose knowledge of it is of longer standing than my own, I perceived that these creatures its inhabitants, not having as it were the semblance of knowledge or civility, can only be restrained by force ; having, as Scripture saith, a bridle set in their mouths, lest, being left to their own evil devices, they suddenly turn and rend you.   And now, with your pardon, I am somewhat weary of speaking, which in this moist air is a thing trying to the throat and lungs, especially upon an empty stomach.   And you must set my loquacity down to my regard for you Master Secretary, and to my desire that you likewise should acquire that philosophy which in this matter has come to me, though not I may say without some travail both of mind and of conscience.'

With that I thanked him heartily for his good counsel, and for the care he had shewn for my interest ; and, falling back a little, I rode along for the space of an hour or more by myself, meditating deeply upon those things which I had heard, and upon the nature of this Island, which, though in outward shew it appeareth much like other lands, yet must surely carry within it some foul hidden Blot or natural Poison, which has drawn upon it the just wrath of Heaven, so that all things that are done for its good turneth to its ill.

For not alone now, but howsoever deep into the abyss of time we peer and penetrate it would seem to have ever been the same. For as the vexed Bermoothes is never still even in the calmest season, so this Land of Ireland has never known peace, neither under the rule of its own chiefs, nor yet under the rule of those governors who came over to it from England. And in all truth and simple gravity it seems to me that unless through the justice and interposition of Heaven it could be speedily sea-swallowed, and engulphed in those waves which eternally rage against it, and thereby converted into a harmless Salt-pool, tenanted with fish in place of men, I much misdoubt it ever will!

VI

UPON the 12th of May his Excellency advanced
to the assault of a castle held by one James
Fitz-Pierce, of the family of the Geraldines, and
passed his forces over the river Barrow.

Here the vanguard advanced upon that portion
of the town of Athy which lies to the South bank
of the river, while the main body forded the same
almost a mile below, so as to be able to attack the
castle on both sides at once. His Lordship the
better to direct the movement of the forces, remaining meanwhile himself upon the bank of the
river, and we of his immediate attendance remaining with him.

While we were still standing there Lo! a
great company both of horse and foot was seen
to approach along the banks of the river. And in
front of the troop rode that noble Lord the Earl
of Ormonde, who had newly come out from Kilkenny to join his forces to those of his Excellency.

With him were about 700 foot, and 200 Irish horse, for the most part very ill caparisoned, likewise two Lords, the Viscount Mountgarret and the Lord Cahir, both of them Butlers, who had previously joined themselves to the rebels, the Viscount Mountgarret being even married to the daughter of the Capital Rebel and Traitor Tyrone, and of closest and most intimate council with him.

Then his Excellency the Lord Lieutenant, after he had advanced a few steps, greeted the Earl of Ormonde with all courtesy, but looked darkly at the other two Lords ; who on their side hung back somewhat, while the Earl spake for them in a low voice, interceding with his Lordship to receive them into favour, they, he said, repenting greatly of those treasons by them aforetime committed.

As he spoke the two Earls stood together, horse by horse, upon the bank of the river. But his Excellency—being anxious for the right assault of the castle—gave after awhile scant heed to the discourse of the other Earl, which he perceiving, grew dark with wrath even to the chin, he being of a swarthy and choleric complexion, and little understanding that anyone could heed ought but his own discourse ; holding himself, as he did, after the Queen and he that was appointed her Lieutenant, the chief in this land of Ireland.

So—looking darkly at the castle—' Methinks my Lord of Essex ' quoth he ' the rebel James Fitz Pierce is minded to hold his castle stoutly in your Lordship's despite ! Perchance 'tis better, that so no excuse may remain for sparing him, as hath oft been done before to the no small loss of her Majesty. And I trust, when your Lordship shall have taken the castle, that you will make an example of him, and command his head to be set upon his own gateway, and his garrison given to the sword ; for all this breed of Geraldines are a pernicious and pestilent race, and there will be no peace in the land till they are rooted out, as their kindred the Desmonds have already been.'

At which his Lordship—looking with a stately port at the lords of Cahir and Mountgarret—

' By my faith my Lord of Ormonde,' quoth he ; ' it were well there were no others beside Geraldines that were rebels ! Methinks such words seem strange in your Lordship's mouth, who did but now intercede for two of your own name, who, if fame belie them not, are as notable rebels as any that this land hath recently bred.'

Then those two Lords, overhearing or suspecting what was said, endeavoured to make
excuses ; saying that it was necessity that had
compelled them, and that all Ireland, saving the
towns of Kilkenny and Dublin, had submitted to
Tyrone, and they but did like the rest. But
my Lord would not hearken to them, and, calling
aloud for the Provost Marshal, desired him to
take them into his keeping, till such times as
he was at leisure to decide what steps to take in
their matters.

But James Fitz Pierce—seeing that the passage
of the river was effected, and his castle so encompassed that it were sure to be taken—presently
delivered both it and himself into the Queen's
hands, praying only for life, which the Lord
Lieutenant granted, (though little deserving was he
of the same), and having put in a garrison to hold
the castle, he entered Athy, and there abode two
nights to allow of the provisions and ammunition
to come up.

So soon as the victuals had come my Lord
commanded that there should be given to each man
four days' provisions, to be carried upon his back,
so that no further danger of scarcity could befal
them, and this done we made all haste towards the

fort of Maryborow [1] in the Queen's County, with
intent to relieve the English garrison there, which
was sore pressed and like to have been forced to
yield. When we entered the passage of the Barrow, which is called Blackford, a party of the
rebels, being chiefly of the sept of the O'Moores,
were gathered together upon the further bank as
if to dispute the passage, numbering perhaps 200
horsemen and twice as many foot. These being
the first rebels I had seen in the open I felt at sight
of them no small curiosity. There were gathered
together in a great cluster the horsemen, wearing
head pieces, and jerkins or jacks, and all carrying
spears in their hands, which shone in the sun.
Nevertheless their arms and legs were for the
most part bare, and they used neither stirrups
nor saddles, but only pads or cushions ; a barbarous and unhandsome mode of riding which
still prevaileth in Ireland, despite many enactments
to the contrary.

When our avaunt guard had passed through the
water and had come out upon the other side, we
fully expected that the rebels would have attacked
them. This they did not do however, but galloped
away ; whereat we rejoiced not a little, seeing that

[1] Maryborough.

they dared not confront us, and so made all haste to Maryborow.

Now when we were still two or three English miles distant we saw the fort rising above the level country, having no flag displayed, nor any sight of soldier or other living thing, so that we greatly feared it had already fallen. But, when we had got within quarter of a mile, I, looking closely, perceived the figure of a man upon the battlements ; who walked, not like one who expected succour, but with his head bent upon his breast, and seemingly in great despondency of soul. He, suddenly lifting his head, looked across the plain, and beheld our army marching towards him, and barely now ten pistol-shots away. At which sight he stood staring, like one in a dream, not knowing whether that which he looked at was real or not. Which, I telling my Lord, he commanded trumpets to be blown, and the rear guard to advance, which was done with all speed. And, we coming to the fort, the gates were flung widely open, and great rejoicings made of all the garrison therein, they having of late looked for nought but a speedy and a most bloody Death.

VII

HAVING plentifully re-victualled the fort and
strengthened the garrison, next day the army
marched away, and, proceeding by Ballyknockan,
reached the edge of a great forest, where his Lordship halted, and with his chief officers ascended
a small acclivity, so as to endeavour to ascertain
where the rebels were posted, and in what strength
they lay.

Through the midst of this forest, which now
lay immediately before us, lay a passage or roadway cut clear ; upon which roadway was no sign
of life, neither of man nor beast, yet we knew
for a certainty, from what our scouts had informed us, that the rebels were posted here in
great force, only so concealed by the trees and
brushwood that it was impossible for us to discern so much as the nose or the hoof of one of
them.

The name of the said passage is the passage of

Cashel, and the forest through which it is cut is known to be one of the chief fastnesses of the rebels in these parts, and the one on which they chiefly rely. The passage itself is a part of the main road called the *Bohermore*, and is about ten going paces wide, the wood on either side thick, and the branches of the trees greatly overlapping the passage. Further to gall the army on its route, the rebels had plashed—so 'tis called—the woods upon either side, which plashing is done by means of the interlacing of boughs, winding them in and out of one another, and where they are naturally scanty, filling them in with fresh boughs cut from the trees, the lower part being made additionally strong with logs.

Knowing that the rebels lay there, and as we had heard in great force, it was held expedient for the army to move warily. Accordingly orders were given to the musketeers to flank the pikes, and the archery to fall in with the wings of shot on either side, and all to proceed in due order, and not more than ten men abreast.

Perceiving in the looks of the men no great signs of spirit, his Excellency rode to and fro in front of the army, encouraging them with his voice, and urging them to show of what mettle

G

they were, and by no means to be discouraged, remembering of what proud nation and breeding
they came ; and that it were a disgrace for English
soldiers to show disquiet before a set of half-
naked Irish kernes and savages.

'What, Gentlemen !' cried he. 'Shall it be said
that you, many of whom took part in the late campaign in Spain, whereby our arms did win such
glory, shall show less mettle upon so much smaller
an occasion? By St. George of England let it
not be so reported of us !' At which words they
raised a shout in reply, yet not so loud or valour-
ous a shout as I have oft heard upon similar
occasions.

Then the avaunt-guard, being ordered to advance through the passage, did so. But, seeing a
clear space not far distant on the other side, and
the forest itself being so dark and evilly menacing,
(though as yet we had seen none of the foe) the
soldiers advanced more and more rapidly, until a
full half of them were through ; whereupon the rest,
perceiving this, pressed on more and more, so that
the order in which they had set forth was not a
little broken. Suddenly, with a great roaring noise,
more like wild beasts than men, the rebels rushed
from their concealment, climbing over, or creep-

ing through the densest parts of the thicket, and falling upon the soldiery like so many Devils new come out of Hell; which sudden assault so scared our men that they stood awhile trembling and astonished, not knowing what manner of foes they had to deal with. Then, the darts which the rebels rained upon them coming ever more and more fast, and many falling, they began to hasten on all together, so that a clear space was soon left in the middle of the forest. Whereupon the rear-guard, being thus cut off, appeared in its turn to be overcome with dismay; the rebels having got between it and those who had advanced into the open.

Seeing that they wavered, his Excellency, cry-ing aloud 'Follow me Gentlemen!' set spurs to his horse and galloped along the passage into the thickest of the enemy, cutting down right and left all that opposed themselves to him, whereat they rapidly gave way, feeling doubtless as if a God rather than a man were dealing Death amongst them, we following also and doing the like, each in his own measure, smiting, and slaying all who tarried to oppose us. Despite of all that we could do, his Lordship nevertheless still kept ahead, so that for awhile there was a clear space between

him and us.   Which reminded me of the first time
ever he witnessed swords crossed, having then but
16 years of age, when he accompanied my Lord
of Leicester, his step father, to Flushing in the Low
Countries, a town of which Sir Philip Sidney was
then governor.   For he and the other young gal-
lants of the army (Sir Philip Sidney himself foremost) were wild to cross swords with the Spaniards,
and a fog coming on not far from the walls of
Zutphen [a town which my Lord of Leicester
desired to capture, and the Duke of Parma, then
commanding the Spaniards, no less desired to
relieve], we, being under Sir John Norris with
1,500 horse, came unexpectedly upon a large body
of Spaniards.   And the night being so thick we at
first knew them not, but no sooner did we do
so than my Lord, plunging madly amongst them
with his sword brandished, was lost from our
sight.   Whom we pursued, fully expecting to find
him dead, so fierce was the charge and so recklessly
had he adventured his life.   Nevertheless by God's
grace he escaped with little more than a sword-
cut across the right arm, which disabled him for
some days, but proved of no lasting injury ; a
mercy the more signal seeing that this very attack
before Zutphen was rendered ever memorable by

the death of that illustrious soldier, poet, and glory
of England, Sir 'Philip Sidney, who, having his
thigh broken by a musket ball, died a few days
later, to the inexpressible grief not alone of his
friends and countrymen, but of the whole World,
and of all that esteemed him one of its Chief
Ornaments.

But to return to these our Leinster rebels,
being so soundly dealt with they did not, I
warrant, long await more such hearty payment,
but retreated with all haste to the forest, taking
refuge there, like four-footed beasts of the field,
which know their own hiding places, to which
hiding places it is scarce possible for Christian
men, unless aided by blood-hounds, to pursue
them.   From beginning to end the whole engage-
ment lasted as nearly as I could calculate not more
than some sixteen or seventeen minutes.

Next to the Lord Lieutenant there was no
one that bore himself that day better than young
Frank Gardner.   For when the first great rush
was made by the rebels he was at some distance.
Nevertheless, seeing his Lordship start, he set
spurs to his horse, and, forcing it to gallop at its
utmost speed, almost succeeded in attaining him,
and was throughout the nearest that followed

him. Then for the space of some three to five
minutes, there was great confusion, swords flashing, darts flying, so that I wist not myself very
clearly what was happening, nor could distinguish
friends from foes. But when this first confusion
had a little abated I saw Frank Gardner setting
his horse at that great wattled fence or plashing
which hemmed the roadway in on either side,
and, having forced it to leap over, he set upon
the rebels, who had now mostly got to that side,
his sword flashing over his head like some young
St. Michael in a Church window. Then for
awhile I again lost sight of him, being somewhat
hotly assailed myself, when all of a sudden Sir
Conyers Clifford passed me at the gallop, his
sword streaming with blood to the very hilt, and
—' See to thy young springal' cried he, pointing
to the wood, ' or of a surety he will be slain.'

Then I looked, and on the other side of the
plashing saw Frank beset with two half-naked
rascals, wearing thick leather doublets, and seemingly naught else, but of so dour and sinewy an
aspect that they scarce seemed to need armour.
Who, having Frank at a disadvantage, the wood
being so thick that it was impossible for him
properly to exercise his horse, were like to pull

him from the saddle. Seeing this I forced my
horse in its turn to leap the fence, and coming to
his rescue we together assailed those two naked
rascals, who, being taken on either side, presently
yielded up their lives, their bodies between us
being served with at least a dozen sword-cuts
apiece. Which—though a pleasant enough entertainment at the time, we both escaping from the
adventure without a scratch—it breaketh my heart
now to recall, remembering how that day, so fairly
entered upon, ended.

For after the combat was over, Frank and I
were riding together along the edge of the forest ;
and the boy was filled with pride and gladness,
because of the good fight, and because he had
acquitted himself well under the very eye of his
Excellency. ' 'Tis the only life !' cried he ' The
only life ! and all other but a mere phantom
image thereof ! And for my part I would gladly
give up every acre of land, till I had left myself no
more than would fit into a lark's cage, rather than
be kept mewed on the same, as my mother would
have me to be ! Marry, that would I, though
I had to trail a pike for it with the meanest soldier
in the army !'

' Be not too sure, or too glad for all that

Master Frank!' said I 'for he that fighteth, the day will surely come when he too will be slain, and eat the dust, as did yonder sturdy rogues late slain by us; yea though he were as strong as Hercules, or as brave as Sir Hector of Troy, so that it may be, not Life but Death, that thou so clamourest for, and desirest to have.'

With that he laughed aloud in the pride of his heart, standing erect in his stirrups, and waving his arms; his hair shining like ripe corn along the edges of his beaver. ' And if it *be* Death ' cried he ' I had liefer die fighting the Queen's enemies than at home in a bed with the quilt up to my chin! Only, being so young, I do hope to have a good many years yet, and a fair stomach-full of fighting, or ever I come to my end.'

At that moment, and even while he yet spake, there came a great shower of darts from an ambuscade wherein certain of the rebels had lain treacherously hid. Most of which fell wide of us, so that at first I thought no harm done. All at once, looking round, I saw Frank Gardner reel in his saddle, and his two hands scrabbling in the air, as though he were trying to seize something, and with that suddenly he fell, and his horse, being affrighted at such a sudden falling, started, and its rider's foot getting entangled in the stirrup, he was dragged after it over the grass many perches distance.

Whereat, wild with fear, I flung myself suddenly from my own horse, and, rushing up to his, caught it by the bridle, and so stopped it. But when I had got the lad clear of it he lay like an image of wood without life or movement. Seeing therefore a soldier pass, I despatched him swiftly for some water, which, when it came, I threw over Frank's head, whereupon he sighed and opened his eyes and—' Tell my Lord—' said he, and struggled to utter somewhat, only the words came not. Then he lay a while, the blood flowing swiftly from a wound which was in his side, and again he muttered something, but all sounded hollow and confused, and like words said brokenly in a dream.

Then, having called for aid, we bore him swiftly back to the camp, and laid him upon a bed. But when the doctor had come, and had examined his hurts, he shook his head, saying that one of them was in a very vital part, and that save for some solace, there was little to do. Nevertheless that night he regained his consciousness, and seemed to be in a fair way, speaking clearly, and strongly,

and with a good courage, and telling me not to
be disquieted, for that he would shortly be as well
as ever.

Next day, the army having to proceed, we laid
him upon a litter made of sticks, which was borne
by 4 soldiers, the same offering their services very
willingly, his gallant conduct the day before having
been so loudly bruited throughout the whole army.
And at first he talked gaily, yet after awhile
suffered greatly from the roughness of the ways,
so that towards afternoon he grew light-headed,
either from the pain of his wounds or from the
fever which they engendered, and, though he talked
and muttered continually, there was little that I,
although the nearest to him, could understand.

When night came, there being no beds to be
procured, we laid him upon an heap of cloaks in a
small tent which my Lord commanded to be set
for him some little way from the noise of the
army.   Here he lay, at first quietly, as if asleep, I
sitting beside him, and no one else near.   Presently,
hearing the sound of a bugle for the collecting of
the men that had strayed, he began first to mutter,
and then to sing some scraps of song, which he
had doubtless caught from the soldiers—' Hark !
Hark ! ' said he—then, after a pause,

> ' Hark ! Hark ! the pipes and drums !
> Rat tat tat tat ! the soldier comes ! '

Then for a space he lay quiet again, and after
that began another stave, or perchance a fragment
of the same,—

> ' Over the rough, over the smooth ;
> Over the rocks and gravel !
> Over the living, over the slain ;
> On the soldiers travel !
> Rat tat tat tat, and Rub a dub dub ! '

And with his poor hands, which had already
grown so weak, he beat upon the cloak which
covered him, as if he were playing upon a drum
or tambourine, such as soldiers use when they are
a marching.

Then—my heart being torn to see him so gone
from himself, and no longer knowing or heeding
me—I was moved (perhaps foolishly) to endeavour
to attract his attention. Yet could I in no wise
succeed in winning him to know me, for his eyes
stared constantly out through the opening of the
tent into the forest beyond, so that it seemed
as if he were watching the birds—small finches,
throstles, and the like—which were going to roost
with some little noise and twittering among the
branches. Presently he began to talk again in a

quick muttering voice, yet withal clearly, calling
upon sundry, whom by their names I knew to be
servants, either of himself or of his mother ; and
especially upon one Ben Brace, who was his chief
henchman, and had been with him since his birth,
and had taught him all he knew of falconry and
such like.

'Ho! uncouple me the dogs, Ben!' cried he.
'Not Dewlap, for he ever overruns the game, but
Spring, and Harkaway, and old Silvervoice, who is
the trustiest brach of the pack.'

Then it seemed that he held himself to be
hare-hunting or stag-hunting, for he began to holloa,
though with a voice so weak that it went to my
very heart to hear him.

'La! La! Yellowface! In for him then, old
wench. In my pretties! There he goes! there
he goes! Hist, hist! for'rard, for'rard!'

Again he grew silent awhile, but ever more
and more restless, tossing himself to and fro on
the bed and flinging aside the cloaks and other
weeds which I had laid on him. Yet still his talk
ran of dogs and of hunting, so that it was plain he
held himself to be at home in Somersetshire, and
once he put out his hand as if to pat some favourite
which pressed against him. And—'Care her well

for me while I am in Ireland—' I heard him say softly, as if to some.one near him.

Suddenly his mood changed again and looking down at his vesture with an air of displeasure,—

' How now rascals ! ' cried he ' How came this spot upon my doublet ? Know you not that I go to the wars with my Lord the Earl of Essex ? Is it fitting that one who is a soldier and a full grown man, and goes to the Irish wars, should have a doublet so besmirched and spoiled ? Nay his Lordship will mock me, and so will the other lords and knights who bear us company, and thus I shall be shamed and discredited, and all for your neglect ! '

Even as he thus spake however, seemingly in anger, his voice grew weaker, and weaker, till I could scarce hear it at all. And—' Oh Hal I am so weary ! ' said he, yet rather as though he spoke to me in some past time than at the present.

The air that night was extraordinarily still, so that there was scarce any sound to be heard save a sort of humming movement from the army, and the cries of the sentries as they changed guard. And several times in the early part of the night one or another would come to the door of the tent, and enquire how the lad fared, for so short a time

as he had been amongst them he had greatly
won the love of all that knew him.   As the night
wore on these nevertheless ceased from coming,
until at length it seemed that he and I were left
alone in a great and solemn vacancy. And whether
he was soothed by this silence, or whether 'twere
through weakness and the fast coming presence of
Death, I know not, but his words, which had
hitherto come rapidly, ceased wholly, and he lay
back upon the couch, and, save that he moaned
from time to time, there was little sign of life.
Then—this state continuing for a long time, and
finding that the moaning also had ceased—I
leaned over him, fearing lest his soul had already
sped, indeed it seemed to me that his breath came
not, and his countenance was white and set like
marble, so that it appeared many years older than
before.   Yet was it a noble and steadfast countenance, seeming to prefigure that man he might have
been, had he in God's grace lived to be a man, and
grown beyond his nonage.

While I still stood there, leaning over him, it
happened that there came a rushing noise of wind
without, so that the leaves in the forest were ruffled,
and brushed one against another, making a soft
noise like the sound of a woman's dress creeping

cautiously along the ground and coming nearer. At that sound Frank Gardner suddenly opened his eyes, and a smile broke over his face, such a smile as one sees upon the face of a little child which has cried itself to sleep, when it wakes suddenly in the night and sees one whom it loves bending over it. And, half lifting his head, he turned his cheek round, as though expecting some one would lay a kiss upon it, (which indeed was fair and smooth still as a maiden's) and with a great sigh full of comfort and satisfaction— 'Mother!' said he very tenderly, and with that word still upon his lips his spirit departed to God who made it.

And I, left there alone by his dead body, fell a weeping and a sobbing like a very woman, and could scarce believe that he was dead, who had seemed to me when alive to be more alive than all others. And 'What? Oh what in God's name?' thought I to myself, 'shall I say to that mother, upon whom he even now called with his last breath, and who doubtless prayeth night and day for his sweet life, little wotting that it is already spilt, and that he lies here, stark and dead, slain without ruth, honour, profit, or comfort by miserable Irish savages, and that too in a skirmish so small and of little importance that men will scarce so much as enquire the very name thereof! '

Towards six of the morning there came one to me from his Excellency, enquiring how the lad fared. And when I returned word to him that he was already dead, my Lord came himself, as did other gentlemen, all grieving greatly for one who had seemed as it were a comely flower or Flag of Youth decking our sad and little joyous company. And many kindly words were said to me of all they that came, they knowing how greatly I cherished the lad, which words I in truth heeded little, being so embruted with my sorrow, as scarce to reckon what befel around me.

That day—the army being upon the road and the time very pressing—we were constrained to bury my dear lad even in that place where he died, and where we were then encamped ; his Excellency sending two of his chaplains to perform the service, and many noble and worthy gentlemen voluntarily attending. For the place, I myself selected it the same morning ; it being very green, fair and smooth, and hard by it there ran a small stream, which, slipping hastily over a short natural declivity, fell with some small noise and bubbling confusion into a tuft or thicket of birch-trees underneath.

And to the right and to the left of the grave itself grew two more young and very slender birch-trees, which I marked, so that I might the better know the place again. Yet were we afraid to erect head-stone, or ought else over him, lest, when we had past on, the savages of the place might, for very despite and wickedness, tear up his dear corpse from its resting place.

Then, the grave being made, we laid him therein, (wrapt in a great furred cloak, which his mother Alas poor soul! had provided to keep him warm and dry on this Irish service) and, when all was over and done that could be done, I requested those who had borne me company that they would leave me there awhile alone, which they courteously did, and retired. Whereupon—seating myself upon a mossy stone which rose out of the ground close to where the grave had been made, and looking towards it—'Oh my lad! my lad' cried I 'Would to God my foolish tongue had rotted away within my mouth or ever I aided thee to come upon this fatal service, or would to God and better still, that I, for whom life at best is but a sorry pilgrimage, were lying there, rather than thou, to whom all things wert bright and fair, and who wert thyself the very brightest thing that walked upon

H

this sad earth's surface!' And in my grief and sore distraction of spirit I must, as it has since seemed to me, have grown somewhat light-headed, for assuredly from time to time I thought that I heard a voice calling to me, and a sound as of steps approaching lightly and blithely across the forest. Yet was there no one there, and no voice whatsoever, only the foolish blubbering of that little stream, which kept leaping, and running, and babbling over its stones, now and then stopping altogether it seemed for a while, then suddenly breaking out anew with a noise like a sob, and hurrying through the reeds and rank herbage which covered that place till it fell over the small declivity, and vanished into the little birchen thicket springing so green and so lush at the bottom.

VIII

HAVING promised the Earl of Ormonde to visit him in his castle of Kilkenny, his Excellency was constrained next day to leave the army, and taking with him a small body of horse, rode thither, I accompanying him with some few others of his household.

Now, for all that there was no great love between his Excellency and the Earl of Ormonde, that nobleman carried it, I must admit, very handsomely, and made great show of welcome to his town and castle, not only to his Lordship himself, but also to all that bore him company. For there was not a man in that town of Kilkenny but was commanded to stand before his house door and bow himself low to the ground as we passed, nor a woman, nor yet a child, even to the smallest, but they must stand at windows, or upon housetops, and wave kerchiefs, or rags of some sort as they could procure them. For the Earl of

Ormonde is in very truth, and in no mere fashion
of words, the Lord of his vassals, so that there
is not one in that town of Kilkenny, no nor
in the whole Palatinate (so they call the region
over which he rules, and of which he is Lord
Palatine) that durst so much as call his very soul
his own, and not rather first his Lord's. Yea
even up to his own near kindred there was not
man or woman, as I speedily found, but trembled
before him, fearing him in a fashion which to our
English notions seems but slavish, and scarce
fitting towards any person save God himself, or
that Sovereign who is appointed as His direct and
visible Vice-regent.

With regard to the town and castle of Kilkenny I can tell little as to their make and
semblance, having in truth noticed little, my eyes
and heart being so bound and blinded with
sorrow, thinking of my poor lad whom I had left
behind me, lying so still in his mossy grave, with
that foolish stream babbling ever beside him.

For as we were coming into the town, and the
trumpets sounded, and the people shouted, and
women waved kerchiefs, I thought to myself 'Ah
how Frank would have laughed with glee and how
his eyes would have danced as he rode along!'

And when the castle was entered and many
gentlemen bravely attired came forward to greet
us, the thought came to me, 'Alas! my Frank
was a braver and a more gallant gentleman than
any of you!' And when we were set down to
the banquet, which was shortly spread before us,
and I saw the great spread of viands, and shew of
wine cups, then I thought 'Ah Frank, you too
would have enjoyed this good cheer!' for he was
ever a valiant trencher-man was Frank, and as
ready with his knife as with his sword, or his
purse either, for all who needed the same. And
these thoughts bred in me such a continual sorrow,
that with difficulty could I refrain from tears, and
my breath came in great windy sighs, so that I
could scarce attempt to set to at the food, but was
forced to leave my knife and fork lying idle upon
the board beside me.

But the lady who had been assigned me to
lead to the banquet, (by name as I afterwards
learned Mistress Alicia Butler, a comely gentle-
woman, though no longer in her May time) seeing
me thus overcome, and like to be choked, took
pity upon me, and enquired what this trouble
was that so miserably oppressed me. Whereupon
I was moved to tell her about my dear lad, and

of his loss which so weighed me down that I could scarce speak, or indeed properly think or breathe.

To all which she listened kindly, with many tender 'Ahs!' and 'Ohs!' and 'Well a days!' such as women use when they are moved to pity. And having told it to her I felt somewhat less burdened, for a trouble which is told weigheth less upon the soul, especially when it is shared with one that is of a ministering spirit, and in whose eyes no less than upon their lips may be read a true and lively compassion.

Finding her so kindly disposed I unfolded myself to her more and more freely, telling her of all that was in my mind, and chiefly of the great trouble and difficulty that beset me in what manner to make known this his cruel grievous death unto my dear lad's mother, who, poor soul, being so wrapt up in his sweet life, and having nought else in this world to cling to, would for a surety fall away and die too if she were told it abruptly, or by one who knew not how to break it to her with discretion.

Then Mistress Butler, having listened to me to the end, sat silent, and, I being about to speak again, she held up her finger, as one who would

say ' Hush ! ' and it was plain to me that she was
thinking earnestly of what were best to do. So I
waited, for that sex—when, departing from its usual
custom, it doth think at all—can often I have
before now found do so with as much purpose-
fulness as we ourselves. Nay it sometimes happens
that their minds, being doubtless less cumbered
with large and weighty matters, do bring forth
thoughts that our solider ones had perchance
scarce lighted on.

So it proved now ; for, turning to me, she said
' Hath not the poor lady any friend, one who is of
like age to herself, and to whom hath also befallen
some such sorrow as this you tell me of ? '

' Truly she has ' I said ' there is just such an
one—Mistress Goldsworthy by name—who being a
long time a widow, did lately lose both her sons in
the wars of the Low Countries.'

' Write to her then ' said Mistress Butler 'and say
that you expect her of her love and friendship to
go to this poor lady, and herself to break and
expound the matter to her.'

' But,' objected I, ' Mistress Goldsworthy, of
whom I speak, hath her abode in the county of
Sussex not far from the town of Lewes, which is at
the least not less than two days' journey on horse-

back from the dwelling place of poor Mistress Gardner.

'Never heed for that, but write to her!' said the lady 'and I will be your surety that no sooner will she have received your letter, and understood what the matter is, than she will straightway prepare herself for the journey, were it ten times the distance. For the heart of one mother that hath been in trouble cleaveth unto another that is in the like plight, even as you may see two drops of water in a fountain cleave and cling one unto the other.'

Then I thanked her, promising to do even as she had advised me, and to write without fail to Mistress Goldsworthy, sending the letter by a sure messenger. 'As for myself' said I 'I shall never dare to present myself again before my Frank's mother, seeing that the sight of me would be to her as ratsbane, or like a fresh wound in her poor heart, knowing that but for my foolish encouragement he had never come to Ireland, but would at this moment be safe and whole beside her.'

'Well' said Mistress Butler, 'seeing that I know not the lady I cannot reply to you positively upon that score. Nevertheless it seems to me that, she being, as you say, a noble and God-fearing

matron, she will bear no such prolonged malice
against you, but will regard you as but an ignorant
and unwotting instrument in the hands of Him
who knoweth what is best for us all. For you
must know Sir, that it is in the endurance of such
woes, as these that the strength and courage of
we women is mainly shewn. For both by nature,
and circumstances we are oft forced to bear, aye
and seemingly to bear willingly, the presence of
those who have wrought us some deadly injury ;
and that too not alone where the said injury hath
been done accidentally and unwittingly as in your
case, but also not unseldom where it hath been
done with full knowledge, intention and understanding of the same.'

With these words she looked, as if constrained
to do so, across the hall to where at the head of
the table sat my Lord of Ormonde, with his
Excellency on his right-hand, and other knights
and gallant noblemen around, he being very stately
in apparel, and erect in port, despite his great age,
yet with a dark, dour, and menacing look upon his
face, so that all who met his gaze seemed to quake
before the same.

I, seeing her so look, fell in my turn to
pitying her, inwardly suspecting that this bread

of which she then eat must at times be but a
bitter crust between her teeth, and that to live
under the gaze, and to submit to the harsh and
sour authority of my Lord of Ormonde (*Black Tom*,
as of those that like him not he is most commonly
called) must to many of his kindred be a sad
and sorry service. And, so thinking, there came
into my mind a tale which I had heard in Dublin,
but at the time heeded little; how two years
since one Pierce Butler had, for some offence
given the State, been brought alive into this very
castle of Kilkenny, and that the Earl his uncle, had
then and there, upon his own sole and absolute
authority, caused him to be beheaded, and his head
sent—not with any special insignia or marks of
honour, such as might in the circumstances have
seemed fitting—but as I was told in a common
hempen bag as a present to the Lord Deputy.

'Truly, and by the Pity of God!' thought I
'supposing the said Pierce Butler to have stood
in some close relation to this poor lady, either as
brother, husband, son, or even as near and dear
kinsman, and that she—all helpless as her sex
naturally are—was constrained, not merely to see
him done to the death without ruth or hesitation,
but afterwards to eat of the bread and drink of

the cup of him that did the same, that were a woe compared to which the worst that could befal a man like myself were light and easy to bear! And this thought was at once both a disturbance and yet a consolation to me. For we mortals are so made that often the best unguent we can lay to our own wound is to be the witness of some still greater and more grievous wound that has to be borne by Another.

That night, as his Excellency was retiring to rest, there came to him a gentleman from Sir Edward Butler, the Earl of Ormonde's next brother, desiring to know if it would please him to hunt the wolf with him next day. Which, he replying that he would gladly do so, the gentleman said that in that case Sir Edward would wait upon his Excellency very early in the morning before the sun was up, when, the wolves, not having yet retired to covert, would more certainly show good sport.

My Lord, who ever sleepeth lightly, was up by three of the clock, blithe as a boy, despite his many pains, at the thought of the sport before him. For my part, I was little inclined that way, being

still so sore of heart by reason of the trouble that
had recently overtaken me; nevertheless at his
desire I rode forth with the rest, his Excellency
and Sir Edward Butler going first with the hounds
and hunters, we that were of his company following
in the rear.

The wood, like most of these Irish woods I
have seen, was very large and the coppices thick,
so that it was not a little difficult to hinder oneself
from being severed from the rest, and I, riding
somewhat carelessly, was soon separated from his
Excellency, and, looking round after a while, found
myself alone, saving only a kerne of the Butlers,
that had been desired to run by my side. For
these Irish kernes will keep up with any horse,
especially in such close and tangled coppices,
where a horseman must needs go softly, lest he
fall unaware into some unseen peril.

The light being still dim I paused, expecting
some indication that would guide me; and, hearing
presently a sound as of a horn, I rode on again,
but after a while came to a place where many
paths forked, and so was brought to a standstill,
not knowing what to do, or whither to go.

With that I made signs to the kerne to go first
and show me the way, whereupon, knowing some

words of English, he replied [whether truly or not] that he himself knew little of the windings of this wood. Accordingly I rode forward again, but slowly, fearing to fall upon some device of the rebels, who I knew thickly beset all this part of the country, coming often in their insolence close to the very walls of Kilkenny, to the no small alarm and disquietude of its citizens.

After about half an hour the sun began to rise, yet could by no means penetrate to where we were, the trees and bushes around being so solid. Yet was there a sweet scent of foliage, and the birds too were beginning to sing blithely in the greenwood, so that the whole world seemed glad and of good courage, as of a morning it often does, let what will have happed at eventide.

We had not gone more than a mile before we heard a sound as of singing, which at first I wondered at, asking myself whether it could be Magical, it seeming to proceed less from a level with ourselves than to be rising up out of the ground below. Nor was it like any singing I had ever heard before, being a strange and gentle cadence, sad and at the same time cheerful, such as rustical folks pretend the fairy or elfin music to be.

Seeing that I paused to listen to it, that kerne of the Butlers made signs to me to tarry where I was, and straightway began to wind and writhe his body through the woods, more like a serpent moving upon its belly than a Christian man. And when he had gone a little way he looked back, making signals that I should advance. So, having dismounted and fastened my horse to a tree, I too moved forward in the same manner, or as near it as I could compass, and came to the place where he stood.

There was a steep pitched bank below us, the ground yawning suddenly away leaving a deep pit or hollow place. In shape it was for all manner of speaking like a Wassail Bowl, such as men send round at yule time, when young and old meet together, and much laughter and merriment is afoot ; the breadth of it some eighty going paces wide, and the depth perhaps twice as much ; the sides very steep, and clothed in brush wood and low timber, save in one place where a great fir tree, having its roots set not far from the bottom, lifted its upper boughs in great tiers one over the other to the very top.

When first my eyes lit upon that bowl I wondered greatly, not knowing if it might have been dug by Enchantment, for it seemed unlikely that the untaught and savage people of the country would have had knowledge and civility enough to dig so great a pit, which would indeed have needed many skilled artificers to open up. Since that time I have learned that such bowls are common in this country, and that they are due to no artifice of man, but to the natural falling away of the soil through the entry of water, which water, lying there, dissolves the ground, and afterwards escaping through holes at the bottom, leaves the pit empty.

At the further end of the pit was a small thicket, somewhat closer than the rest, and, by stooping a little, I could see a sort of pent-roof of bushes, welded together in the fashion of a bird's nest, from which nest or thicket proceeded that sound of singing we had heard. So, making signs to the Butler kerne to make no noise, I waited awhile, wondering to myself who it could be that would inhabit such a place.

Presently there came a stirring about of the boughs, and a woman stepped out from under the roof, bearing a young child in her arms, which she, sitting down upon the bank, began to dance and dandle on her knee, as mothers do, singing to it the while that strange and savage song which we had heard. Whereat the creature laughed, and crowed, and kicked lustily with its legs, which were bare, as was its whole body, save for some sorry rags wound around its middle. Yet it seemed a fair child, of a good ruddy colour and well liking, such as I wot many a childless Dame of high degree would gladly have called by her Lord's name.

It being still so early, scarce six of the clock, the woman doubtless fancied herself alone, and so sang to her babe, which—savage and far distant from civility as she was—she doubtless loved in her fashion no less than they that are of a higher breeding. Her head being turned from me I could not see her face, but her hair was dark and very long, hanging down in loose quantities over her shoulders.

For what cause I know not, save that my heart was perhaps softened and made foolish by sorrow, but the song of that savage woman as she sat with her babe upon her knee, little wotting that any eyes beheld her, went to my heart as few strains have ever done, and I could not but think, as I had done the night before, of the hard lot of those who, without fault of their own, are set in the midst of cruel warfare, and beset with many pangs and perils, which they, being weak and helpless, can by no means hinder or avert.

Of this truth I at that moment had a most lively example, for, hearing by good hap a sound as of a cord strained under the finger, I looked round suddenly, and saw that the kerne of the Butlers had set an arrow in his bow, and was taking aim at the mother and her child as they sat there in the hollow, suspecting nothing.

Then—being filled with wrath at this sight—I turned upon him swiftly, and, seizing him by the throat, caused him to drop the bolt.

' Cur ! Caitiff ! Cruel villain !' cried I furiously. ' Would you slay those that are doing no harm, and by their youth and helplessness seem to cry aloud as with tongues for pity and mercy ? '

Whereat all astonished, as one that looked not for such treatment, he replied, as far as I could understand his language, that the woman was of the party of certain rebels, who often hid their women and children in such places, and that it would greatly pleasure Sir Edward Butler to know that they had been slain.

' Rebel me no rebels, rascal !' quoth I. ' They are women and infants, and are doing no harm to mortal man. An' if I catch you, Master Kerne,

I

playing such devil's trick, beshrew me but I will chop that body of yours into small pieces with my sword or ever your fingers can reach again to your bowstring.'

At that speech of mine he began to writhe to and fro without speaking, doubling himself the while as if suddenly took with the colic. Then, all at once, and before I wist what he was going to do, he slipt from my hands, and shot away, supple as an eel, and fled through the trees, leaving me there alone.

So, being left to myself, cut off from his Excellency and the rest, and in a barbarous and savage country, I was at first in a sore strait what to do. Nevertheless, returning to where I left my horse, and taking it by the bridle I advanced with such speed as I could make, the way being very thick, and all overgrown with briers. There was no path, nor any sign that there ever had been one, nor was there ought to see or hear, saving only the birds, which that day were singing like mad things in the branches, and once I spied a grey wolf stealing past under the covert, which glared at me with glassy eyes, and so vanished again.

Presently I came to a place which was more open, the grass and moist weeds shining like jewels

new set by some ·lapidary, and a small stream of
water running swiftly by in the sunlight. There
was a bank here, overgrown with whins and prickly
gorze, and the ground below it blue as Heaven
with a small belled flower—the name of which I
could not recal, though methought the face of it
seemed familiar and kindly.

Upon this bank I sat down to rest, wondering
within myself what I should do. And, as I so sat,
there presently came to my ear the sound of
whistling, like the whistling of a bird, which
nevertheless was not a bird's voice, though clear
and shrill as one. So I waited, thinking that he
who whistled so loudly must needs be in good
case, and perchance might be one of a company
that could guide me back to Kilkenny. And as
I waited, lo! there came through the trees a boy
some 10 or 11 years of age, having scarce a rag
to cover his nakedness, only a sort of short red
kirtle like a woman's round his waist, and a wisp
of straw or hay about his shoulders, and the rest
of him naked as the day on which he was born.
Then, still making no sound, I was filled with
amazement at the good content of one that was
in such evil plight, for his face was thin and starved
as if with hunger, yet he laughed and leaped in the

middle of the space, all for pure glee, whistling
like a mavis the while.

So I sat, staring at him. Then, moving suddenly, I called to him to ask the way. But, when
he caught sight of me and of the horse, he too
stood for a moment, staring like one that had seen
an evil spirit, and the next he scampered away like
a coney under roots and between boughs, diving
as it were headlong through the midst of the wood,
so that I speedily lost sight of him.

After that I wandered about for some hours,
sore spent and beset with hunger, not having as
yet broken my fast that day, and it was not until
two of the clock that by the mercy of God I
again heard a sound of hounds baying, and shortly
afterwards fell in with my Lord and the rest of his
following returning home from the wolf hunting.

Upon the way back to Kilkenny the talk ran
of wolves, and of those that shewed the best sport,
as the large grey wolf, and also of the smaller dun
one, which two it would seem are the sorts that
chiefly prevail in this country. And, this finished,
the talk branched to hawking, and the divers
varieties of hawks, of which my Lord Ormonde
and Sir Edward Butler have it seems great store ;
and which made the swiftest flight, and which

could strike surest, and which lie longest upon the wing.

To all this I for my part gave but little heed, my mind and ears seeming to myself to be still full of the song of that savage woman I had listened to awhile before. And all that evening many strange thoughts bore me company, nay even at night-time and in my sleep they beset me, I being much burdened by the thought of Mistress Gardner ; with whose image I in dreams confounded that of Mistress Butler, by whose side I again sat that evening, while with the images of both these gentlewomen there mingled, [as even in my sleep I was aware somewhat improperly !] the image of that savage woman, sitting with her baby upon her knee, and singing so solitarily in the woodland.

IX

HAVING taken a courteous leave of the ladies, and thanked the Earl of Ormonde for his good cheer, upon the 21st of May his Excellency left Kilkenny and joined the camp, and next day marched with the army towards Munster, and lodged in a small village called Clanbroghan, and upon the twenty-third came to Clonmel, which is upon the river Suir, where the army rested both to refresh itself, and to await the coming of cannon and munition from Waterford.

At a distance of about five miles from that town of Clonmel, in the midst of this river Suir, stands an island or natural rock, and upon this island a castle, which castle is so strong both by nature and art that it is believed by all Ireland to be impregnable.   Its name is the castle of Cahir, and it is the chief house of Thomas Butler, Lord of Cahir, and a place of greater consequence than any other in this part of Munster, being both a passage upon the river, and also near to the White Knight's country, and to that of the Burkes, called Clanwilliam and Muskerry.

This Thomas Butler Lord of Cahir was at that time with the army, and had promised to yield his castle so soon as ever his Excellency drew near, it being then held by James Butler his younger brother. At Clonmel however high words passed between the two lords, his Excellency suspecting the Lord Cahir of having privily admitted strangers into his castle, in order to make a party for the White Knight, and to hinder its deliverance. This the other denied with oaths, swearing that none were in it but his own kindred only, and further that it should for a certainty be delivered over upon the very next day, and that he himself would engage to go and see that it was so done.

His Excellency agreeing to this, next day sent him and Sir Henry Danvers to draw forth his brother and the ward, and to admit the garrison appointed, telling the said Sir Henry to watch closely what befel. But when these two, Lord Cahir and Sir Henry Danvers, drew near to hold a parley, James Butler refused to surrender the castle, swearing that he would not give up so much as a

stone of it, and bitterly reviling his brother with
many furious words, not alone in the English language, but in the Irish also.

When his Excellency saw them returning, and
the soldiers too that had been sent with them to
garrison the castle, and learnt that it was not to
be yielded up, he fell into great wrath, and called
quickly together a Council, namely the Earl of
Ormonde, the Marshall, Sir George Bouchier, Sir
Warham St. Leger, and the Sergeant Major, to
consider what means were at hand to force the
place.

These being found to be very scant he sent for
more munitions to Waterford, and also to all the
towns round about for victuals for the army. And
this done he called again before him the Lord
Cahir, saying first to those around—'Now look you
well my Lords and Gentlemen, and mark when I
shall challenge this traitor what answer he makes,
and if he seem to palter ; for I am firmly persuaded
that he is in concert with his brother, and that they
two do but play with us ; the one out yonder in
open defiance upon his rock, the other here secretly
within our own camp.'

Then, when the Lord Cahir had come in, the
Viscount Mountgarret who is his brother-in-law

also following him, his Excellency challenged him loudly, saying

'How now! How now, my lord of Cahir, for you must answer for yourself! How comes it that this castle of yours stands at defiance against her Majesty, seeing that you its lord are here in our midst, and do profess obedience?'

Then at the first the Lord Cahir seemed not to know how to answer; presently, plucking up a little courage, 'Verily, my lord, and as I am a Christian man, the fault is none of mine' said he earnestly 'seeing that I besought my brother to yield up the castle, as Sir Henry Danvers here present who was with me can testify, and can tell you how I was myself assailed with many insolent and disgraceful words of those that came out to parley.'

'That is true' said Sir Henry Danvers, 'fouler language did I never hear by one brother to another, and I can testify that the Lord Cahir here present did in words beseech his brother to yield up the castle quietly into your Excellency's hands.'

'Aye' said the Viscount Mountgarret 'for I too was there and heard the words he said.'

With that his Excellency's anger broke suddenly out and—'Words! Words! Words! What

are words ? ' cried he, rapping upon the board with
his two hands, ' I tell you 'tis not words but deeds
that must answer this matter.   Here stand I, and
all her Majesty's army, being kept at defiance and
delayed upon our southern journey by this proud
rebel, and there stands my lord of Cahir, who did
vow and swear, not once but many times, that so
soon as we approached the castle it should be
yielded peaceably.   Did you so swear, my lord of
Cahir, or did you not ? '

' Truly my Lord ' answered the other ' I did,
but——'

' No *buts* sir! no *buts*!' cried his Excellency
loudly.   ' I want neither *buts* nor *ifs*, nor any other
words, but plain dealing and loyalty.   And this I
tell you my lord of Cahir, that though you and all
Ireland believe this castle of yours to be impregnable, yet here I stand, and from this spot I stir
not till I have reduced it, though it took me a
year to do it, aye and the loss of every second man
in my army.   And so you may tell your brother,
and every other fellow traitor of yours under
yonder walls.'

' Fellow traitors my Lord!' said the lord Cahir
tremblingly.   ' I hope your Excellency does not
reckon me with traitors ? '

'Marry do I,' answered his Excellency roundly.

With that the Earl of Ormonde and the Viscount Mountgarret would have interposed, praying his Excellency to send once again to the castle to parley, and not to judge the lord Cahir upon a single failure. While others of the Council said nay but such conduct was clearly traitorous, and no otherwise; and others said first one thing and then another, so that for a time there was great confusion, and no man could hear what any other said, for they all spake together. But his Excellency turned angrily from them all, and would listen to no more question of parleying, but called to him the chief engineer, and commanded him to make ready his battering engines, and the chief petarger also to prepare his petars, and all things to be got in readiness for the siege.

Next day, the artillery having at last arrived, a bank was cast up within fifty paces of the castle, and a platform made for the cannon. Gabions too were set up so as to cover the gunners. The culverin was placed somewhat further off, where it might see more of the flanks of the castle, so as to beat down the sights. All being ready, at the first dawn of day the cannon began to

play, with a great roaring noise and a tremble-
ment of the ground, which did greatly terrify the
besieged and all that heard it ; and then would it
for a surety have broken down the walls but that
by an evil chance its carriage broke at the second
shot, and could not be repaired in less than a day
and a half.

This causing again great delay, and finding
that the rebels went in and out of the castle at
their pleasure, his Excellency sent three hundred
men under Sir Thomas Gates to take possession
of a small orchard lying close under the walls.
He also despatched men in boats to drop upon
another island or rock a little lower down the
stream, and further boats to carry victuals, so
that they might remain there until the castle was
taken. The great Sow was got in readiness to
advance upon the besieged so soon as ever a
sap was made in the walls, while at the same
time Sir Charles Percy and Sir Christopher St.
Lawrence, with four old companies that could
be trusted, were bidden to hold themselves concealed, but ready to rush in under cover of the
culverin, and to take possession. And this proved
the most important disposition of all, for, whether
it was that these great preparations broke down

the spirits of those that were within, or whether they hoped to escape where none would look for them, certain it is that that very night the garrison made an attempt to save themselves by a sally, but were so well received by Sir Charles Percy and Sir Christopher St. Lawrence that only a few escaped by swimming, under cover of dark, the rest being all put to the sword.

The castle being thus cleared of its late evil tenants, was straightway entered by his Excellency ; the cannon and culverin were brought in, the breaches repaired, and a garrison placed in it under the command of Colonel George Carey.

All that went in that day, of whom I myself was one, were greatly astonished at the strength of the place, it being so favoured by nature and so cunningly laid out by art that forty resolute men might well have held it against four thousand. But truly the strength of the Wicked is but weakness, and their guile folly, so that when they think themselves firmest then are they the nearest to their fall. And, this matter being brought to so happy an ending, upon the next day the army marched thence, and encamped on the last day of May near Cashel, and upon the first of June we entered Limerick, where his Excellency proposed to remain some little while, both to prepare for the further transport of the army, and also to recruit his own health, which had greatly suffered in the late toilsome and uneasy marches.

X

AND now may all men see whether he spares himself, as his enemies declare, or not! Scarcely had he reached Limerick than word was brought to his Excellency that the Queen's garrison at Askeaton was sore distressed, lying in the midst of the rebels and in great want of victual. Whereupon, despite his own fatigue, and despite the newness of his arrival, nought would do him but he must hasten at once to its aid, the rather that the pretended Earl of Desmond had sworn, it was reported, to impeach his passage.

We set out accordingly on the 4th day of June, being accompanied part of the distance by the Earl of Clanricarde and Sir Conyers Clifford, whom the Lord Lieutenant had given command to repair to their several charges.

For some way out of Limerick our road lay over a wide plain, for the most part wooded, the cleared places bare and sorry to look at, and the ground scurvily covered with short grass, whereas upon the other side of Limerick the grass is of a richness rarely to be seen, more especially in those portions called of the natives *corcass*.

Three miles out his Excellency halted on the side of a small stream, running swiftly between tall banks, and waited till the two gentlemen that were to leave him came up. And, having first dismissed the Earl of Clanricarde with good words, he advanced to meet Sir Conyers Clifford, who was following with Sir Alexander Ratcliffe, and reached out his hand to him, saying—

'Truly, Sir Conyers, I am most loathe to see you go! For I may tell you that there is none in all this army that so strengthens my heart as you do. And, but that the Queen would have it so, you were better methinks by my side than in yonder remote Presidency of yours, which is scarce worthy the time and attention of such a man as thou art.'

'Nay, nay, my Lord' says Sir Conyers sturdily. ''Twere best I go, seeing that it is her Majesty's pleasure.'

'Aye, aye' echoed his Excellency somewhat bitterly. 'We must all do her pleasure, be it for our own banning, or even for hers also!'

With that they looked steadfastly into one

another's eyes for the space of some minutes. His Lordship sitting erect on his horse, his head held high as his wont is ; Sir Conyers Clifford with his face all wrinkled, as though it had been sat on by his nurse in cradle, but a good face withal, and a soldierly.

'Well fare you well, my Lord, till we meet again, and God be your guide' said he. With that he turned, and rode away to the Westward, and the other knights after him, the sun—which for a wonder shone that day—glittering fair upon their morions and breastplates. And little I dreamed that I should never see his gallant face again. Yet so it was, for he and most of those that were with him that day were slain miserably one little month after by certain ragged O'Rourkes and O'Donnells in the passage of the Curlews in Mayo, as must in due time be told.

But my Lord rode very silently on towards the South. And twice as we were going I heard him sigh, and twice he muttered something, I know not what, only that the name of Sir Conyers Clifford was in it I can affirm. And after a while we left the cleared places behind us, and once more came to great woods, and to bogs full of large and white-shining pools of shallow water.

K

Here—knowing that the pretended Desmond and his following were lying somewhere close at hand—his Excellency gave orders to advance with all care, especially as it grew dusk, lest, gathering their courage in the darkness, they should fall upon us when we were least prepared, and so do harm in the confusion.

That evening the sky was of a wonderful clearness, the western portion of it becoming towards sunset inflamed with a pale reddish hue. Southward lay a large grey cloud which somewhat stained this clearness, looking like smoke from a cauldron, but below it the sky was again ruddy, of a clear transparent ruddiness, as it were a lamp set behind a screen of alabaster. A sadder region, or one more disposing the mind to dolorous thoughts I have never seen ; the trees being for the most part exceedingly old, and bent as if like to fall ; the pools below them of a dull whitish hue, save where the pattern of the branches crossed them in a black entanglement.

Having seen to the disposition of the army his Excellency again rode on a little ahead of the main body, only the avaunt guard being about three lengths ahead of him, and the rest about as

far behind. Presently turning to me, who still kept
nearest to him—

'Strange stuff we are made of, Master Har-
monius!' said he rather low, and as if not
wishful that others besides myself should hear
him. 'And strange thoughts visit and invade our
minds, especially when the body is somewhat
distempered, and our thoughts therefore, being
looser, come in and out like wild birds without
leave or license. Know you that often as I ride
over this sad Earth of Ireland the thought rises
to my mind that all these that follow behind me
are but a train of the Dead that ride thus, and I
their Ghostly King. Dost understand, Oh poet,
that there are moods when a man's life seems to
himself but a phantom, as it were a picture sun
shining upon picture men? moods in which the
grave with its writhing company seems to be the
one reality, and all else falsity; nay when one
were almost glad that the rest were over, and that
reality come?'

Then—being surprised at such words from his
lips—I was moved to answer strongly

'Nay my Lord' said I 'such talk is surely contrary to reason, if I dare with reverence say so
What evil destiny or danger of death is there for

one whom the Queen's Grace loveth to honour as herself, and whose fortune and merit standeth so high as hath scarce happened to any subject in our times ? '

Then he laughed a little, as his way is, and smote upon his horse's neck with the flat of his hand.

' Faith Hal,' cried he, ' the Queen's Grace has as you say been but too gracious, and has doubtless raised me to a higher estate than any other in this her thrice delectable Kingdom of Ireland.   Still, so gracious as she is, she is a woman, and a sovereign, to boot, and sovereigns are to subjects as we to these lower creatures that do serve us.   I love Suleiman here, yet were he to stumble and fall, through no fault of his, but because a spear flung from these traitorous Desmonds had wounded him, should I cherish him, think you, as of yore, and make of him still my chief warhorse ?   Nay I should leave him, I fear, to fare as he could, with these savage woods for stable, and wolves for grooms, and would forthwith mount another horse and go on.   For a man's life is more than his horse, were it the noblest that ever champed bit.   But when I spoke of doom I spoke rather of that doom which waits for all of us, were we even

crowned kings. Know you that often since we set
forth from Dublin, aye even in the thick of fighting
and when the kernes were flying hard before us,
and I, being in the front, did with the rest smite
them down, as a reaper smites corn with his sickle.
Even then, as my sword descended upon some
half naked fool's head, and his blood spouted hot
and fast under the blade, the thought would pass
through me—' Well knave, there thou goest, and
I who sent thee am but the poorer and sorrier
knave of the two! For thou at least hast suffered
thy last pang, and thy last terror, and thy last
misery, and all is over with thee, whereas I have
I know not what still to endure, and am the
sport of those who from on High behold us, knowing what our end shall be, of which end we ourselves know nothing, nor can by any effort of ours
discern so much as the least hint or fragment of
the same.'

Then I answered nothing, for the truth of his
words struck like iron to my heart, knowing that
none are so high but what ill may come to them,
especially one who like my Lord hath all his life
lived in the thick of moving chances and hot encounters, and whose very nature it is to draw danger
upon him, as a magnet draws the needles. And

so we rode along, more like two monks muttering
paternosters than a great lord and chief of an
army with his following.   And about eight in the
evening we came to the castle of Adare, belonging
to the Earl of Kildare, and set in the midst of great
woods and bogs.   Here the army had to encounter
certain of the Desmonds, but having forced its
way past them, and entered across a wooden bridge,
it encamped there for the night.

Early next day, being informed of the way by
the guides, we again entered the woods.   Hardly
however had the advanced guard got in than
the rebels discharged upon them a volley of shot,
which so discouraged them that they turned and
would have fled, but that his Excellency, reproach-
ing them openly for their cowardice, urged them
forward, and with the aid of the Marshall and the
Earl of Thomond, who that day led the Forlorn
Hope, pushed them through with the loss of about
100 of the rebels and 20 of ours, and so came to
Askeaton ; [where the following day being the
Sabbath] we rested, and sermons were by his Excellency's orders read by the chaplains in every
quarter of the camp, to the great refreshment of
all that heard them.

Now what I have at present to relate, is of so

strange and unnatural a character that were it in a tale all would crý out upon its improbability. Nay even I, who am witness of the same, would scarce to dare relate it, but that, before leaving Ireland, his Excellency strictly charged me to write down everything that occurred upon this our journey, to the end that he might have a record of it; seeing that such a record, he said smilingly, would be pleasing to read when he came to be an old man. Which age may God grant in his mercy that he attain to, and not first be cut off and overcome on the way by those that like ravening wolves thirst after his dear life to destroy it!

That day the army, as afore said, rested, his Excellency's own quarters being laid in an old monkery, belonging to the late traitor Earl of Desmond, whose chief lands lay hereabout, lands now forfeited to the Crown, but wrongfully and insolently usurped by the false Earl of Desmond, called in mockery the *Sugane*, or Straw Earl. This monkery of Askeaton stands at a little distance from the castle of the same name, both rising very solitarily in the midst of great champion fields, reaching out for many miles upon one side, while upon the other lies a great forest, stretching down nearly to the banks of the Shannan—not Shenan

as Mr. Spenser in his poem improperly calls it—
a great and mighty river, fit to convey all the
ships of war in the Queen's dominions, but upon
which no boats are to be seen save certain small
and unstable vessels called of the natives '*cotts*,'
which are used for the conveyance of fish and other
small commodities.

The watch being set, my Lord retired to rest,
suffering greatly, as hath of late been usual with
him, from heavy cramps brought on by the wetness of the ways, which he endureth with a constancy that in one of his impatient temper is a
wonder both to see and to know.

His bed was nothing better than a great heap
of straw, covered with clothes, and set at one end
of the monkery, in what had formerly been an
oratory of the Earl of Desmond, and still retained
some semblance of a roof, though much broken
by ill usage ; while upon the further side rose a
tower attained to by a staircase. Being unable
to sleep my Lord desired me to stay awhile beside
him, and, leaning upon his elbow, he discoursed of
many things ; some sorrowful, others of a more
cheerful character, as his mood was. Yet ever his
talk recurred to this woeful country Ireland, of which
in an evil moment he had, so he declared, accepted

the charge ; saying that it passed the wit of man to devise means which would bring it to subjection, unless it were wholly conquercd and destroyed by the sword, and its people rooted out by famine ; as had been done in former times by the Lord Grey, Sir John Perrot, and others, in this very province of Munster.

And of many other things discoursed he, of which I in truth remember little, being in sore strait with the desire to sleep, so that in mine own despite my head sank upon my breast, and his Lordship's words sounded hollow and distant, like the voice of one that speaketh afar off.

Now there was a stone doorway immediatcly in front of where his Excellency was lying, from which doorway a staircase led to the tower, at foot of which tower a sentry was placed, whose duty it was to walk to and fro the passage between the chapel in which my Lord lay and that larger portion of the building wherein other gentlemen, to wit my Lord of Thomond, Sir John Amory, Captain Seth-cock and others were disposed.

The moon that night was nearly at the full, but much obscured with clouds, and shone with a strange steelly glitter, now bright and anon dark, so that it seemed to me to dip and dance in the

sky, as a boat doth upon stormy waves ; nay to
shine now in one place, and now again suddenly
in another ; though whether it really did so, or,
my eyes being heavy, it appeared to do so, I cannot
of a truth say.

His Excellency had already lain down, having
in part divested himself of his clothes, only his
inner coat and hose he still retained, being fearful
of the chill of that place ; a great cloak lined with
miniver being also flung around him to keep him
from the roughness of the ground.

Meseems I must have slept awhile, for what
happened just before I remember not. Suddenly
I felt his Excellency clutch me, and when I looked
up he had reared himself erect in his bed, his eyes
all wide and staring, and with a loud voice he
cried to me to know—Who was That ?

So I turned, fearing I knew not what, and
heavy still by reason of my sleep. And lo ! in
the middle of the doorway leading to the tower
stood a man, having upon him clothes made in
the Irish fashion ; to wit a long dark cloak, which
the natives call a *bratt*, covering him nearly to the
feet, and under it a close-fitting vest of white stuff,
and trews upon his legs. And he, neither going
nor yet advancing, stood there, as though he were

a graven statue, and gazed ever fixedly upon his
Excellency. And his age was seemingly that of
a man well stricken in years, and his face very
hollow and worn of aspect, yet haughty withal, like
one that had endured the last extremity, and now,
for very despair, careth not what befalls him. And
there was a smile upon his lips, such a smile as I
n'er saw before, and pray to God in his mercy I
may never see again ; a smile such as a dead man
might wear when his murderer drew nigh, as the
custom is, and placed his hand upon his breast, and
the blood gushed out before all men for a token.
Yea a smile of pleasure too, as of one whose
enemy is brought low, and who joys to think that
with his very eyes he shall behold some evil and
cruel hap befal him.

So we stood while a man might count ten ; he
facing us all the time. Then his Excellency,
taking up his sword, which lay by the bed, rose
suddenly, and with a threatening look rushed
toward the doorway. But when he was about six
paces from it he stopped, and began to shiver
greatly. So I looked, and lo ! there was nothing
to be seen, only the stars and the moonlight.
Nevertheless a rumbling noise as of distant thunder,
seemed to me to fill the air, coming from a

great way off, and dying slowly away toward the river.

His Excellency, coming back, stood silent for a while; then motioned to me to call the sentry who was at the foot of the tower, and when he was come near he asked him saying—'Didst see any one pass?'

Whereat the man looked bewildered, like one that had been roused from sleep, though he stood erect before us. And he answered No, that he had seen no man pass.

'And did you hear nought?' said I; for the noise of that strange sound seemed still to be in our ears, so that methought the very air rang and trembled with it.

To this the man answering nothing, I looked again, and saw that his eyes were closing, like one that had no power to keep them open; his mouth too opening and shutting strangely, as if of itself.

Seeing that his Excellency waxed suddenly angry, and, seizing him by the throat, shook him to and fro, so that the pike which he carried rattled and fell to the ground.

'What ails you sirrah?' cried he. 'Art drunk? or dost think the work of guarding the Queen's

Viceroy so trifling a task that it can be done in this neglectful fashion ? Dost not fear for thy life, lest thou be shot for a traitor, and an aider and abettor of traitors ? '

While he was yet speaking, suddenly the same sound was in both our ears, and with it a shock as if the ground had opened ; and a great and exceeding rumble like thunder, yet not like any thunder that ever I heard.

Then his Excellency, loosing hold of the sentry, motioned to me saying, ' Come up with me, Hal, into yonder tower, for of a surety I will find out whence came yonder man, and for what purpose he presumed to trouble us this night.'

When we had got up into the tower, which was of no great height, being approached by only some 30 steps, we came out on to a flattish space above. And at first we saw nought, save the level country, looking all grey in the moonlight, and the forest, stretching darkly away as it seemed to the confines of the earth, and that great river the Shannan spreading westward like a broad lake or inland sea. Below us the ground was deep with fog, which lay in an uneven manner over the land, gathered as it were into packs, here a space bare, and there another covered to the depth of many feet; and so thick and solid that it seemed as if one might walk thereon.

Then, as we stood looking out over it, lo! that fog seemed to cleave into two parts, as we read in Holy Writ that the Red Sea was cleft; and a passage appeared down the midst thereof, which passage seemed about two going paces wide, and at first to be utterly void of all life or movement. Nevertheless, after my Lord and I had stood awhile looking at it, behold! a stranger, and a more terrible sight was seen. For all along those pathways which, when first we saw them were, I say, devoid of life, it presently seemed to our eyes that a great multitude of people were beginning to pass, and to approach that castle whereon we stood. Though whence they came God alone knoweth, for there was no place for them to come out of, neither village, nor habitation of any sort; all this country round Askeaton, (which was in former times I was told somewhat thickly peopled) having been utterly destroyed in the last wars, first by Sir Nicholas Malby the President of Connaught, and afterwards by my Lord of Ormonde and Sir Henry Pelham; who utterly levelled all habitations, both small and great, slaying the people, and destroying the harvest and beasts of the field, so that it remains waste and void unto this day.

Nevertheless I who write these words do hereby solemnly take oath that I did with mine own eyes see that great multitude of people advancing directly towards us. And as they came nearer I could plainly distinguish one from another, so that it seemed to me that only a small portion of them were full-grown men, the rest being women or children, gathered into companies, each company by itself, some in sixes or sevens, and some in tens as it served. And in each group the children went first in a little band, and after them a man and woman side by side, or sometimes two or three women, and in the rear followed the aged people, both men and women, some of these so old and feeble that I was amazed at the sight of their skinny faces, which seemed to be those of skeletons rather than of living men or women. With regard to the fashion of their raiment I could see little, by reason of the fog and obscurity, but methought they were such as are worn in this country, the more so that many appeared to have scarce on any raiment at all, only sorry weeds hanging around them ; but, whenever I tried to distinguish anything clearly, all at once it seemed to melt away into that fog out of which it came.

Now, when I saw that sight, and those long trains of figures—formed as it were out of the mist of the ground, yet moving one after the other, and having limbs and bodies like other men— seeing this I am fain to avow that I stood like one in a trance, trembling in every limb, and the hair of my head began to rise, so that I felt the bristling thereof, and my heart was as a weaver's shuttle, running to and fro in my breast so that it scarce allowed me time to breathe.

Then, glancing at his Excellency, I saw that he too was much moved at that strange sight. Nevertheless his cheek kept its usual colour, and he gazed steadfastly at what lay below.   Now there were others who had been aroused by the noise ; to wit Sir Thomas Egerton, Sir Henry Danvers and some more gentlemen, who had recently come up upon another wall which ran immediately below us ; and with them it seemed to me that I discerned another figure ; which figure was grey and tall, and moved along with a slow stately pace, rather gliding as it seemed than walking, till it stood right in front of us.   Suddenly I heard the voice of Colonel Sethcock, who had just then come out upon the same portion of the tower upon which we stood. And he, crying with an exceedingly loud voice, exclaimed—'Christ Jesus have mercy upon us! Yonder is the Desmond himself.'

'What Desmond?' asked my Lord, turning sharply round to him, and speaking quickly. Then —seeing that he made no answer, only that his teeth chattered like one in a palsy, so that no words could come through them—

'What Desmond?' repeated he sharply.

'The old Desmond' replied the other, only rather like a man in a dream than as if he understood rightly what he said—'him that was slain at Castlemain in the county of Cork.'

'And if that be he,' said my Lord, 'who in God's name are these?'—pointing to the crowd which still moved below.

To this Colonel Sethcock answered nothing, and we, gazing at him, saw that his face was ghastly as the faces of those below; and much I misdoubt me but that the memory of some deed of more than common kind was stirring within him, else had he never looked so wan and terrified, like a man upon whom some ill, committed in his life and thought to have been left behind, had suddenly sprung up again to confront him.

L

But at last—' Who are they your Excellency ? '
said he with a sort of break in his voice, and upon
his face, for all its terror, an evil smile. 'Your
Excellency asks me who are they, when there were
an hundred and thirty thousand—men, women, and
children of all degrees—slain or died of famine
during that time, and if their spirits wander to this
day is that my fault, or shall their deaths be accounted to me as a sin more than to others, who
did even as I did, or is their blood more upon *my*
head than upon the heads of other men ?   Is it my
fault I ask ?   Is it *mine* ?   Is it *mine* ?   Is it *mine* ? '

These three last words shrieked he louder and
louder, waving his hands, and stepping back as if
to wave away some that pressed upon him ; though
there was nothing that we who stood nearest to
him could see.   And at length, still waving his
hand in the air, he fled along the battlement,
shrieking and raving like a man distraught ; we
meanwhile gazing one at another, and wondering
greatly within ourselves what all this might mean.
But when we turned again to the ground, lo !
there was nothing of all that great multitude to
be seen ; only the moonlight shining upon the
stunted bushes—sorry blackthorns, sloeberries and
the like—which rose up here and there out of the

flatness ; nay the very fog itself had melted away, so that we could see to the confines of the ocean, and all so void of life that it seemed certain that what we had seen had been no other than a phantom of the night, created doubtless by the craft of evil spirits, such as Scripture saith walk about seeking whom they may devour ; of which sort this distracted Land has, I dare affirm, a larger number than most.

'Gentlemen' said my Lord, seeing that all stood trembling and astonished, 'we have seen a strange sight, and meseems 'twere fitting we retired to meditate thereon, and to compose our minds ; so that we be not shaken out of our Constancy, by ought that may occur ; commending ourselves to Almighty God, in whose hands we and all things, whether terrestrial or superterrestrial, live and are contained. And so I dismiss you to such rest as you may obtain, which I for my part purpose also to seek.'

With these words, he saluted them very nobly, and descended the steps ; the other gentlemen retiring also, every man to his own quarters. Nor was there any more disturbance that night, neither sight nor sound ; only a moaning of the wind, which seemed to wander sadly round those ruined walls, set in the midst of so great a desolation. But next morning when I enquired how Colonel Seth-cock fared, I learnt that on returning to his own quarters he had fallen into a great swoon, with much groaning ; and so continued all that day and the next, so that we were forced to leave him behind us in the charge of a few soldiers ; nor did he, as I afterwards learned, know anyone for a full fortnight more ; and ever since then, (now some three months) he moaneth and shivereth, they say, like one that hath something upon his mind, and is so shrunk and wasted as to be scarce recognizable of those that knew him aforetime.

XI

SEEING that nothing of any note happened for some time, I will for brevity's sake set down here what I find entered from day to day in the record kept by me at my Lord's desire ; in which record I each night wrote down that which seemed of most moment in the day preceding.

June 4th. My Lord set forth for Crumme castle, belonging to the Earl of Kildare, and lay there with all the army.

June 6th. This day during a skirmish was slain of the rebels one Burke, a great rascal, and on our side Sir Henry Norris, whose leg being broken by a bullet, after severe suffering he died, greatly regretted of the entire army.

June 7th. This day came by messenger letters to his Excellency from the Queen's Majesty, at reading whereof my Lord seemed but ill pleased.

June 8th. Rain fell heavily all night and his Excellency's encampment was like to have been washed away. The straw on which he lay being too wet to sleep upon, my Lord sat up and read the Essays of Montaigne until the morning.

June 10. His Excellency sent letters by certain messengers who went post to Court with them. Divers of my Lord's people were put on pensions to live at 5 pence a day, or else return to their friends.

June 11. His Excellency took one of the rebels' castles and razed it, slaying divers who had concealed themselves therein, but sparing two women ; of whom there had been seven, but the rest were by some accident slain with the garrison.

June 30. A spy brought in and hanged.

July 4. A girl who had warned divers rebels to escape brought in by a company of soldiers. After examining her his Excellency commanded her to be set at liberty, whereat was much dissatisfaction amongst certain of his council, who would fain have seen her hanged.

July 5. This day, being Sunday, his Excellency rested at Ballingar, at an house belonging to Sir James Devereux. Mr. Prettyman the chaplain in ordinary preached. His text was the I Epistle of S. Peter ; the 5th chapter, and 5th verse. ‘ *God resisteth the proud, and giveth grace unto the humble.*’

After the preaching his Excellency knighted Sir
John Barrington and Sir Michael Foster. Heads
of Mac Dermot Oge and Turlough O'Toole
sent in.

July 10. Last night after the watch was set
an alarm was raised ; his Excellency himself rising
and coming out, supposing it to be some treacherous surprise of the rebels. There was a great
panic in the camp, certain of the soldiery crying
out that the O'Tooles were amongst them, others
the Macarthys, and others they knew not who, only
that some foes were there they were sure. The
army having entered into quarters late that night
the confusion was very great ; the ground too
upon which the camp was pitched was very wet
so that many slipped in the mud, or fell over
great stepping stones set hither and thither in
the pathway. Being so dark, and the rain falling,
torches were hastily lit ; which same seemed but to
increase the confusion, being reflected brokenly
here and there in the pools of water. So strange
a scene I have scarce beheld ; men running wildly
hither and thither, many of them wellnigh stark
naked, having pulled off their clothes to dry them ;
and all in the confusion taking one another for the
Irish, so that they were like to have been slain,

only that weapons, happily, were scant amongst them.

After the confusion had continued for a long time, and many been bruised with falling over the stones, or striking one another in their haste, it was found that the enemy was nought but a great herd of cows, belonging to those rebels in whose houses we lay ; the said cows having been driven by the women into the mountains, and having of their own accord returned to their former quarters, they being, in the savage fashion of this country, wont to lodge in the same house as their owners. Which cause being ascertained, order was at length restored, and the army returned, somewhat shame-facedly, every man to his own quarters.

July 12. This day we crossed the mountains, which though of no great height are yet difficult to traverse by reason of the great slipperiness of their rocks. Leaving the army on the road to Fermoy, his Excellency with an hundred horse rode to Mallow, and lay that night at the house of the President of Munster. Here he was met by the Lord Barry with 60 horse, also by a gentleman of the English Pale, by name Mr. John Delahide, who, having much property in Kerry, had been constrained for the safety of his goods to appear to take part with the rebels. He—pleading the urgency of this need, and his own sorrow for the same—was by his Lordship received into favour, the rather that he was a gentleman of good address, speaking English as few in this land speak it, yet withal well acquainted with the country. Whom, keeping beside him as he rode back to camp, his Excellency discoursed much ; seeming to be better pleased with him than with any of this land's breeding he hath yet encountered.

After quitting Mallow we again crossed a portion of the great woods, in which we were met by the rebels, and at a skirmish at one of the passes Sir Henry Danvers was shot in the face, but seems like, the doctors say, to do well. His Excellency purposed lodging that night half a mile short of Conna, but, finding the houses there had been burned by the rebels, he lodged the army betwixt Conna and Mogeelly, and slept himself at a castle which one Mr. Pine holds of Sir Walter Raleigh. This castle being better furnished, and fitter for entertainment than most of the places he had lain in, his Excellency invited the Lord Barry to sup with him ; also Mr. Delahide, with the President of Munster, and other gentlemen, besides his own accustomed following.

The dinner over, and the gentlemen gathered to wine and discourse, there entered one who whispered something to Mr. Delahide; whereupon, addressing his Excellency, he told him that an old Irish harper stayed without, and would he allow him to come in, and give the company a specimen of his quality.

This his Excellency permitting, they brought in the harper, who was in truth a man very old and venerable to look on; having a long white beard which fell to his breast. His clothes were of green flannel, made after this country's manner, belted in at the waist, and falling below the knee. His legs bare, only for short hose of wool, and his feet shod with shoes or buskins of wolf skin; the hair outside, tied with two thongs across the instep, the toes and heels flat, and the name of them, as I understand, in the Irish tongue '*pampooties*' or '*pampooters*.' His head was also bare, the hair on it of a snowy whiteness, falling heavily over the forehead in a *glibbe*. For his face it was well writ over with the map of his age, only the eyes still dark and fiery; and the look of them very strange, being both fierce and timorous at once.

His harp was larger than any harp I had yet seen in this country, standing some four feet from the ground, and painted a lively green colour with sundry devices, and traceries of curious significance; also leaves and other ornaments, but all much bleached and defaced, doubtless by rough weather and the evil usage it had met with.

He—coming forward in a lull of the discourse —bowed himself low to the company, especially to his Excellency, who sat at the head of the table. And immediately he began to stray his fingers lightly over the strings, running from one to the other, and looking about him, fearfully yet confidently, as if to ask what was wished. And that strain he played reminded me of the song that I had heard sung by the wild woman in the hollow place of the wood, the morning that I rode forth from Kilkenny with the Butler kerne, and lost my way in the forest. And, having come to an end of it, he paused, and looked round from one to another, as it were from under the pent-house of his brows, which for all his age were black still and very thick.

Then certain airs were commanded, which he played ; and afterwards Mr. Delahide said some words to him in the Irish tongue, urging him to play or sing something ; at which he shook his head, yet it seemed to me reluctantly, as if he would fain have done that which was required of him, only durst not.

'What asked you of him?' enquired his Excellency, who like myself had observed this commerce between them.

'I desired him' replied Mr. Delahide 'to sing a dirge, which he himself had composed, and which in times past I have often heard him sing, in honour of one Rory Oge O'More, whose harper, or *Senna-chie*—that being the Irish word—he formerly was, which of all pieces writ in the Irish tongue seemed ever to me the most moving, both for the words and the air thereof.'

'And who or what was this Rory Oge O'More?' asked his Excellency 'for meseems his name is familiar to me.'

'As vile, dangerous, and pestilent a Rebel as ever this land, which is rich in little else, hath bred!' cried the President of Munster. 'And I wonder that Mr. Delahide would even name him in this presence, still less desire songs in his honour to be sung before one who stands as our Queen's Viceregent, and before whom the countenancing of such songs is a clear insolence to her greatness.'

'Yet, methinks, as the song in question is in the

Irish tongue, and that none here save myself, and possibly you, my lord President, know ought of that language, it were scarce perilous to the loyalty even of the least wary to sit and listen to what they could by no means understand!' Mr. Delahide said mockingly, and with a smile upon his lips.

'Marry, that is true!' cried his Excellency. 'Therefore, Mr. Delahide, I charge you to command him to sing this song, about which you have moved my curiosity, and, if danger there be in his singing, I myself will be his surety that no harm shall happen to him for the said cause.'

His Lordship having so spoken, Mr. Delahide spake a few words again in Irish to the harper; who thereat straightened himself, flinging suddenly off that bowed and dejected aspect he had hitherto worn, and looking a full score of years younger, so brightly did his eyes flash and his whole face alter. And he looked about him now, no longer scared and timorous, but with a fierce defiant air; and especially I noted that he so looked at the President of Munster, as much as to say that he understood his animosity, yet feared it not, having the sanction of one that was greater than he.

So, having turned his harp about, he lifted it a ittle, and set it upon a stool or trestle that stood there; and, placing himself beside it, struck his hands across the strings with a careless gesture. Then, having played awhile, he suddenly broke out into a sort of singing, which yet was hardly singing, but rather a chant or crooning noise, which swelled and swelled so that at times it seemed to rise to the very rafters, rolling and beating about like thunder within our ears, and again to sink till it was no louder than the whisper of a summer stream over grass and small stones; his harp the while seeming to follow and take part, more like a thing of separate life joining in at its own pleasure, than an instrument played by the hands. Stranger singing and playing I never heard before, nor expect ever to hear again.

It chanced that, being next to the window, I saw what was not, I think, seen of others in the company. For when that strange song or chant first began all the kernes, galloglasses, and other wild Irish mustered without started and stared, seeming to prick their ears, as a horse does at the sound of the trumpet. Presently, as it went on, they began to draw nearer and nearer; yea the very bearers of burdens and churls,—creatures seemingly scarce human—gathered, till a score or more were below the window. And I ·marked that they looked one at the other with eyes wide open, as if asking how such a song came to be heard in such a place and before such company. Then—that wild singing still continuing, and rising ever louder and louder—they began to grip at one another with their hands, and to move to and fro with their feet, as if they would fain have broken into wild dancing and leaping. Only, whenever anyone came out of the castle, they all dispersed suddenly ; or fell flat upon the ground, hoping to escape notice in the dark, but so soon as that person had passed on, they rose up again, and crept nearer and nearer, as if their very souls fed upon what they heard !

The evening growing late, as soon as this strange song or dirge was over, and my Lord had dismissed the old man with a fair gift of money, the company broke up ; his Excellency retiring to his chamber. Thither I was about to follow him when Mr. Delahide requested me to bear him company a little longer, he being not yet inclined, he said, for sleep. To pleasure him I remained therefore where I was ; we two sitting down again, close to where a great chimney gaped in the side of the hall, adown which the wind whistled with a shrill complaining sound.

And [by way perhaps of accompaniment to that dolorous music, or to those other wild strains we had late listened to] he related to me, I remember, on that occasion sundry tales which be current in this country; as of Wraiths, and Goblins; of Presentiment, and Tragical Prophecies; also of foul Witch-women who wait on men to announce to them their coming Doom; and many other such bogyish and old-wife tales, which, though devoid of all reasonable probability, are yet apt to make a man feel goose-skinned and timorous if he chance to waken towards two or three of a morning, and to see the moon peeping whitely at him from behind some corpse-coloured cloud.

When we at length parted he gave me a scroll to deliver to his Lordship; telling me that it was a translation of that song or dirge the harper had sung, which he had himself put into English, and which his Excellency it seems had desired to see. This I promised to do; and—finding on entering his chamber that my Lord had not yet retired to rest—I delivered it into his hands.

Having glanced at it himself, he commanded me to read it aloud, which I did to the best of my powers, the handwriting being very crabbed, and the story a confused and bombastical invention, setting forth with many savage illustrations the greatness and glory of this Rory Oge O'More, and the treachery by which his end had been accomplished; the said tale or invention, I own, interesting me slightly.

But his Lordship apparently took it otherwise, for he remained musing awhile after the reading was over. And at last—

'Did the thought ever come to you Hal' said he suddenly 'that 't were well these Irish— especially such as are given to the composing of similar songs and dirges—should not be acquainted with the English tongue, or indeed with any civilised and current language?'

'Credit me, no, my Lord' said I. 'On the contrary it seems to me that the best hope of their ceasing from their savagery lies in the learning of them our own tongue; were it by compulsion, and the punishment of such as fail to acquire the same.'

'For their sakes perchance, Hal, but 'twas rather of our own I meant.'

'Ours? my Lord' said I 'how could the acquiring of English by these savages work us either good or ill?'

'In this way Hal. Think you if such a tale as you have just read to me were put into some

M

language current among men of letters 'twould produce no effect upon those that heard it?'

'Faith, my Lord' said I 'it seemed to my poor judgment to be a wild and heathenish sort of composition, not pertaining to any recognized progression of words, whether of prose or poetry, but a confused and disorderly admixture of both.'

'For the form, Hal, I bow to thy superior authority! For all that it seemed to me as I listened, and especially as I recalled the looks and gestures of yonder harper in the hall, that 'twere as well for our credit that we alone had the exposition of our quarrel with this people, and not they theirs also. And of this I am sure, that were I born an Irishman, and given to the poetic craft, I could tell such a tale as would send every maid that heard it weeping to her bed ; aye and might chance to leave behind it not a few of those Tragedies by which our London stage has of late been held.'

'That your Lordship,' said I gravely, 'is not an Irishman (which to suppose even in a jest seems to me I own profane) is no doubt fortunate. But, with regard to those that are such by birth, methinks there is little fear of any such thought visiting their minds; they doubtless knowing themselves to be as inferior to us by nature as they are by birth and breeding, a circumstance which is to all men visible and manifest.'

'Oh Hal, Hal! Least imaginative of poets!' cried he, shaking his hand at me, ''Tis little, trust me, good Pomposity, we know about such matters, or can so much as guess at the thoughts of others, especially of those we despise ; contempt being as it were a natural veil or blinder of the eyes, hindering us from guessing how they whom we scorn do in their turn regard us. What says Montaigne—" When my cat and I entertain each other with apish tricks who knows but I make to my cat more cause for sport and derision than she does to me ; nay who knows but it is a mere defect of my not understanding her language that we agree no better ? " '

These words of his Lordship—which at the time, I own, seemed to me fantastical—came back to my memory a few days later. For as we were on the road to Waterford it chanced that there broke out a violent quarrel between Sir Henry Sudley, newly made knight after the skirmish near Askeaton, and one Major Morrison, who had expected knighthood at the same time, yet had not hitherto received it. And, whether this disappointment rankled in his

M 2

mind, or whether some earlier quarrel was brewing between the two gentlemen, certain it is that a vehement dispute arose, each man laying his hand upon his sword, and both uttering many despiteful words ; whereupon others of their company joined in, some on one side, and some on the other ; so that it seemed as if the matter thus begun was like to grow to a formidable size and aspect.

Now it befel that I, riding at the time somewhat in the rear, chanced to cast my eye upon certain of the kernes who carried the provisions, of whom —horses being scarce—there were then with the army great numbers. And, being near enough to see their faces, I noticed that they looked eagerly one at another ; their eyes gleaming, as if well pleased at this quarrel so suddenly broken out, and hoping that it might go further. An observation which at first surprised me not a little, it seeming scarce natural that creatures so debased should take any note of what went on before them, any more than if they had been in reality beasts of burden. For as Porphyry shows that there is a scale of creatures rising through the lower animals to ourselves, and through us to the Heavenly Essences, or Angels, so it had always seemed to me natural to regard these native Irish as intermediate betwixt us and the lower animals, having the outward form of man, but in all higher matters no share of his heritage. A mode of regarding the matter which I now perceive may be carried too far, and might even lead to a foolish and heady arrogance, seeing that they are in truth humans like ourselves, as are also the Red Americans, and other lowly races ; a reflection which 'twere well to keep before the mind, so as to avoid the sin of arrogance, and to preserve our souls in a state of due humility, as becometh Christian men.

XII

OFTEN, when there has been question of the Irish
service, I have wondered to hear men cry out
against those woods with which so much of the
surface of this country is still covered.   And that,
not husbandmen merely, or rough persons, who
for gain's sake naturally love a clear soil, but even
those who, like poor Mr. Spenser lately dead, might
be expected to take a livelier and less self-bounded
view of the matter.   For 'tis plain, thought I, that
forests are in themselves pleasing things ; being gifts
from God to man, given both for coolness in the hot
season, and also to afford the means of kindling a
fire, and so keeping in the natural heat of the body
when winter is at hand, snow falls, and the cold
winds, howling over the earth, turn blue his cheeks,
and make his courage to feel as nipped and as
numb as his finger ends.

Since I have myself been in Ireland however,
especially since this journey that I took with his

Excellency through the forests lying around the mountains called Galtimore or the Galtee, I have come to view the matter otherwise, and to understand many things which formerly surprised me. For these forests—stretching nigh 'tis said from sea to sea—give harbourage to every kind of noxious beast, of which the least noxious are the wolves (which in some portions abound terribly, slaying all who travel alone through it), and the worst are those foul pests and curses to humanity called the Wood-kernes or Wood-caterans ; who, being protected themselves by the density of their thorny thickets, dwell in safety, and at night, like wolves, only far more wickedly, sally out to destroy all that be not of their own nature and kidney. So that I can now well understand that saying widely spread abroad, and to be heard upon every loyal lip, namely, that ' Ireland never will be conquered while the leaves are on the trees,' and do hold it part of true policy and sound wisdom to cut down these same traitor-harbouring trees wherever and wheresoever they can be got at ; seeing that it is better plainly to have a naked land and obedience, than a well-covered one filled with such godless Runagates and Haltersacks.

Having greatly suffered in its passage through

the southern portion of this forest, it was with the
more satisfaction that the army attained a somewhat clearer place, standing upon the slope of the
lower hills ; where the camp could be set out free
of the bushes, which be the lurking places of these
scurvy thieves, and whence they creep out privily
when none expect them. His Excellency's tent
was set at a little distance from the camp, so that
he might enjoy more privacy ; and having sent
out a party of horse to burn certain villages belonging to the tribe of the O'Dwyers, he retired to
rest, trusting to enjoy some sound sleep ; a restora-
tion to which he hath of late, unhappily, been too
commonly a stranger.

Early next morning I was by his orders at his
tent, it not being yet six of the clock, but the sun
already high, and the birds singing lustily. I found
him already risen, having spent a good night, and,
the morning being unwontedly fair, he was moved
to go out, and desired me to accompany him ; an
order which I with all readiness obeyed.

At this place a kind of green lane or track
led into the heart of the forest, somewhat poached
in portions by the recent tread of horses, but withal
firm and pleasant to walk upon. Indeed it was
strange to see how fair and serene all looked, so

that even we, who knew how far from the reality
that semblance was, could scarce forbear being
beguiled by it. Nor would anyone, seeing it so
solitary, have believed that a great company of
men and horses were gathered so near at hand ;
for though from time to time we could hear the
buzzing sound of voices, and the jingling of bridles,
or the rallying note of a bugle, yet 'twas so mixed
and broken that the finches, merlins, and other
dainty Chanters of the wood could readily be
discerned above it all.

Then—the scene being thus solitary, and my
Lord seemingly little disposed to speech—my
mind was moved to meditations, such as come to
a man at such times, and chiefly I thought of my
dear lad Frank Gardner, who had travelled over
to this land so blithely, nothing doubting that
he would win fame and honour, and who now lieth
dead under this Irish sod, that looks so fresh and
fair to the eye, yet carries within it so many a
bloody corpse, both of those that belong to the
land, and those that have come over to subdue it
and bring it to civility.

So thinking, I sighed several times heavily,
which sighing attracted his Lordship's attention,
who had hitherto walked along silently, stroking

his beard from time to time ; his coat of cinnabar
velvet (for he had not yet put on armour)—looking
like gold in the rays of sunlight ; his whole gait
and port so noble that it was a wonder to see.

'How now, friend Harmonious?' quoth he,
'whence these sighs which seem to be tearing thy
heart in twain ? Sure this sunlight, which rarely
lights us in so blithe a fashion, might inspire merrier
thoughts than seem to be inflating thy bosom.
Nay, as I look again, thy countenance is even
more dolorous than its wont, or than thy garb—'
(which that day was plain black, only the sleeves
slashed with white silk above the elbows).

'Alas, my Lord,' said I, 'I was thinking of poor
Frank Gardner, who, your Lordship knows, was
ever to me as a young brother, and whose death
lies sore upon my heart ; the rather that but for
my foolish aid he had never come hither, but
would be standing safe on English sward, the joy
of his mother, who, poor lady ! is, as your Lordship
is aware, a widow, and hath no other son than he
of whom she is so cruelly bereft.'

Then, with that kindliness, which, more even
than his great qualities, binds men to him, his
Excellency laid his hand upon my shoulder, softly,
as a woman might.

' Faith Hal' said he ' I might have guessed
whither thy thoughts, poor faithful one, had gone,
and so have spared thee the question ! Well I
know how thou enshrinest that lad's memory in
thy heart, nor do I blame thee, for a gallanter
youth never eyes rested on, or one that would
have made a better soldier had he been spared to
come to man's estate. Yet remember this, good
Hal, Death cometh to us all, and spareth not any
place, the safest and securest no more than the
very battle field ; therefore lay not that evil chance
to thine own score, as if through fault of thine it
came about. Bethink thee too how many lives
are better than *un bel morire* ? For this big word
Death, about which we make such a pother as if
'twere the only ill in the world, only think of
what a sea of ills is it the cure. For what says
Francis—" Revenge triumphs over it, love slights
it, honour aspires to it, grief flies to it." Again "a
man would die " says he " only from mere weariness
to do the same thing over and over." Or if you
will not heed Francis—whom for all his wit I know
you love little—list to the ancient poet, who tells
us that no security will so case a man but what
some dart will find him out ; " for he may arm
himself" he says " with steel and brass, yet Death

will pull his head out of the helmet!"—with which
citation I will e'en bring my discourse to an end,
seeing that my eloquence savours somewhat of
pedantry.'

So saying, and losing go of my shoulder, his
Lordship advanced at a quicker step, as if to give
me no time to relapse into any more such vapourish
musings. Now we had just reached a small knoll
or hillock, rising out of the plain ground of the
forest, which knoll he ascended, and I with him.
As far as I could see it was part composed of
rock, very grey in colour, and of a softish texture,
and upon the top rose a small group of trees,
their trunks large, and còvered with moss, hanging
down in bags. The earth—as throughout this
portion of Ireland—was reddish brown, and of a
boggy quality, the greater portion of it covered
with a small-leaved plant of shrub-like growth
giving out under the foot an aromatic odour, and
called for this reason, as I have learned, *Bog myrtle*.
A comelier spot I have rarely seen, the sun-light
falling slant-wise betwixt the trees; the small heaths
and other forest flowers shining gayly; as also did
certain young shrubs of birch which sprouted here
and there, the bark whereof was of a shining
lustre, like freshly woven satin, and their leaves so

green and so daintily set on the stalks that they
seemed to flutter at every breath.

My Lord took note of all this, smiling a little
as he looked around him, and at last—'Truly,
Hal, Ned Spenser was right when he called it a
fair land and a goodly as any under Heaven!'
cried he. 'I know not why, but there are moments
when my heart seems to yearn to it, for all the
plagues it brings me; moments when I say to
myself that I would gladly serve it, were it for any
time or in any office, if I could thereby hope to
bring it to peace and prosperity at the last.'

'Every man, my Lord,' replied I gravely, 'has
it seems to me his own office upon earth appointed
to him, like the stars which shine in the heavens,
and are not permitted by any means to change
their order. And for remaining in this country,
only consider how poor Mr. Spenser was himself
forced to flee from it at the beginning of the
late troubles, nor did he escape without loss of
all that he had acquired; so that for grief and
disappointment he has himself since died miserably.'

'True,' answered my Lord sighing. 'As that
knave Raleigh says, it is indeed a " loste land," and
he that thinks to bring peace to it will only bring

woe upon himself, and in no wise mend that which seems beyond the power or wit of man to heal. And yet, Hal, it seems to me that the best way of dealing with this people has not been found, though what that way is, beshrew me if I can tell you!'

Then—just as I was about to point out how many noble gentlemen had taken pains to that end, yea our gracious Queen herself had not spared her own labour—suddenly there came a sound of horses' hoofs and a clinking of bridles, and looking up we saw, coming two by two through the forest, —for there was not room on the path for more to go abreast—that troop of horse which my Lord had sent out the night before.

Seeing us standing there, and perceiving all at once that it was his Lordship, the foremost of the riders—a Colour Sergeant by name Johnson, a man out of Lincolnshire—turned in our direction, and, riding up, saluted, bridling in his horse, and waiting for his Excellency to speak; the other men of the troop remaining a few paces behind.

Then his Lordship, straightening himself, looked at the man, and addressing him, said—

'You executed my orders Sergeant?'

'Verily we did, my Lord.'

' And did the men whom you were sent after resist ? '

' Faith, my Lord, we gave them scant opportunity ' replied the fellow. ' For we caught them napping like foxes in their burrow, and have even made a clean end of the whole brood ! '

' Had they no watch then ? ' enquired his Lordship.

' If they had, my Lord, the sentry rascals were asleep, so had no chance to play us any of their scurvy tricks, for their heads were off their shoulders like the 'rest, ere they had well shaken from them their drowsiness.'

Then—seeing that his Lordship frowned somewhat, as if scarce as well pleased with the tidings as might have been expected — the Sergeant beckoned to one of the troopers who rode immediately behind him, and across whose saddle as I had already noticed hung a great leathern sack, such as farmers use for carrying grain, and before we fully understood what his purport was, he had taken it from the man, and with a blunt— ' Your Lordship will see whether we have misspent our time or not ! '—he turned it over on the grass.

And lo ! there rolled out of it a score or more

of heads, which—there being at that place a little declivity, or falling away of the ground, and the heads of their nature round—they fell and slid one over the other ; rolling on and on to the foot of that knoll on which we stood, much as though they had been balls sent in some game of bowls or rounders ; until—that impulse which projected them being spent—they lay amongst the grass and flowering weeds, which half hid them, yet not so completely but what they and all the ground about were freaked with drops of blood.   And some of the heads appeared to be those of old men, the hair grey or scanty, while others were young and smooth of face, and one belike was a woman, for its hair was long, and all seemed to stare amazed, as if the poor carrion wondered greatly what had befallen it, and had scarce yet got over that confusion and amazement in which it had died.

Then—looking at them as they lay there, gazing up as it seemed with glassy eyes—I could not but be for a moment moved to see so many fellow creatures, who—let them be never such rebels—had lain down last night, nothing doubting but that they should rise again in the morning, and were now for ever utterly stark and cold.

Nevertheless that in so slaying them, even in their sleep and unawares, we rendered them no other than their deserts is certain. For as rats and similar vermin must be slain when and how we can find them, so also traitors, and those who rebel against God and their sovereign. For see how David, who was the man after God's own heart, scrupled not to surprise the Philistines in their sleep, or Jael, who slew Sisera in her own tent, and was upon that account regarded as a glory to her people, although but a woman. Which things are clearly written for our example, showing that in dealing with a froward savage people we must be guided, less by those precepts which prevail betwixt civilized men, than by those fortunate gifts of cunning and strategy whereby we are enabled to triumph over the strength of savage beasts, seeking them in their holes and dwelling places, and there smiting them, lest, being left untroubled, they, from very ferocity and bestial rage, turn and rend us.

But my Lord—having stared awhile upon that red carrion lying so quietly at our feet—turned and strode suddenly back with long steps to his tent ; uttering no word, either of praise or of blame.

After waiting awhile, finding that he did not

N

return, I followed him, and found him pacing to
and fro with an air of no little disquietude.

'Are you ill, my Lord?' I asked, for his face
seemed to me paler than usual, and his features
were discomposed, like those of a man seized with
some sudden distemper.

'Am I Hal' said he, 'Troth I know not what
I am, or rightly who I am!' And with hasty
steps like one distraught he continued to pace
to and fro the tent while a man might count an
hundred.   Suddenly turning to me—

'Tell me Hal,' cried he "am I a boy? a
whipster? a fool?   Come, answer quickly! am I?
am I?'

'My Lord' said I, 'my Lord! who dares say
such things of your Lordship?'

'I asked you not who says them, but I asked
you am I?   Now in honesty and fair speaking, as
a friend and not a servant, tell me—am I such a
poor, sickly, puling thing?'

'No my Lord' replied I readily, 'nor ever
were, not even when in age you were but a
stripling.'

'Then why is it Hal—expound me this, Oh
excellent Oracle, if you can—why is it that what
disturbs not other men — soldiers, God-fearing

gentlemen—disturbs me. Disturbs? aye sickens
me! fills my soul with loathing, so that my senses
seem to cry out with one accord, and my very
stomach heaves as 'twere like to vomit.'

'You speak, my Lord,' said I hesitatingly, 'of
yon ugly sight we just left behind us in the
wood?'

'Aye Hal, of that and of many another ugly
sight that hath met me since I set foot in this
thrice-cursed, this infested, sin-beridden land of
Ireland! But since I assuredly made not its
troubles, why, I ask, should I heed them, seeing
that others trouble themselves not with the same?
My father—God rest his soul—put a score daily
to the sword where I have put one. Did he sleep
the worse for it? or was his soul when he came
to die perturbed on that account? Not so, he
parted calmly as a Christian man should, at peace
with God and all the world. My lord Grey—
who would fain, as 'twas said, have made a
Mahometan conquest of this whole island, and
have dyed its very seas red with the blood of its
people—was his soul burdened on that account?
Not so again! rather he counted what he did well
pleasing in the sight of the Almighty, they being
not alone such rank Papists, but the sworn friends

N 2

and abettors of the king of Spain. Nay, if he re-
pented of ought, 't was that he had not, while
chance favoured him, rid the earth of more such
froward caitiffs! Then, why I ask you Hal, should
I—saving for some womanish weakness or folly
that I carry from my mother—feel thus perturbed
and sickened by what other men heed not?'

'Your nature, my Lord' said I, 'is of a more
poetic texture than was that of my lord Grey, or
even of the late illustrious Nobleman your father,
and poetic natures as they have higher joys than
others, so they have this disadvantage in dealing
with the grosser things of life that many crosses,
unheeded of rougher souls, jar and fret them, as
small unevennesses in a palette disagree with
tender skins, yet hurt not the coarser ones.'

'Pish Hal!' cried he impatiently, 'thy apology,
worthy friend, savours of the courtier, and of
courtiers, God wot, we have enough and to spare!
And for this daintiness with which your politeness
endows me, 't would never sure for a moment
compare with that of the illustrious poet, incom-
parable knight, and flower of all chivalry, Sir
Walter Raleigh, who, an he be not greatly maligned,
did such deeds in this very forest in which we be
standing, that 't is marvel the trees carry not his

sign-manual written in blood upon their trunks as a memorial for ever ! Nay, believe me, we deceive ourselves grossly with such words, attributing to the finer side of us what is far oftener some ganglion astray, some defect in our bodily structures, than any such over fineness of mind or spirit. Certes 'twas no air-fraught daintiness such as you would ascribe to me, but a plain honest heaving of the stomach that overtook me when yonder bloody-fingered knave tumbled out his spoils with such glee, and the blood ran in a red rain to our feet. But enough ! The fit is past ! No more o' it, in God's name ! no more ! Go bid the trumpeters sound ; 'tis time we were on the march. Essex is himself again, and will let no more such whimsical follies—born perchance like goblins or pookas out of the quagmires and pestilential swamps of this unhealthy land—come between him and aught that he has to do. What ! shall fifty naked rascals be slaughtered in their sleep, and our Excellency's stomach turn at it ! A truce upon such folly ! Forward ! and the devil take any traitorous bile that would dare rise and spoil our appetite again upon so pitiful an occasion !'

Yet, though his Lordship so spake, and though throughout the rest of that day he was cheerful above his common, I, who know the thoughts of his heart, perceived that a secret distaste still clung to him, and that much, that to another would be but customary, was to him irksome almost above the bearing. Moreover it seemed to me, as I watched him closely, that he set his thoughts ever more and more from that day towards getting rid of this uneasy governance, and returning with all speed to England, to which resolution I, alas ! in no small degree ascribe much that afterwards befel, nay much which—save God in his Good Providence do avert it—may yet be to befal.

XIII

Now falls it to my unhappy lot, (I being a true, if humble historian, and not a mere dresser-up of pretty lies like some who undertake that office) to recount the deep disgrace and sore mishap which befel her Majesty's troops under the command of Sir Henry Harrington, the news of which was brought to us in this wise.

Leaving the thickest part of the forest, my Lord marched to Affane on the Broad water, through a great pass by Lisfynnen. And at Affane we had to cross a ford, which is only passable one hour before and one hour after low water, and so came to a village two miles short of Dungarvan, where we halted for the night. Here a council was held in his Lordship's tent to consider the fittest manner of pushing on the war in Munster, the President thereof, who sat that day at his Excellency's right hand, vehemently urging the setting up of a sufficient number of garrisons. 'For by garrisons only' said he, 'the heart of these rebels is to be broken.' This advice being by the rest of the council approved, and the garrisons agreed upon, the council broke up, his Lordship remaining awhile longer to conclude the signing of certain instructions for those who were to depart next day to their charges. Suddenly, while he still sat there, a loud noise and disturbance was heard without, and one was seen running hastily toward the tent, having his dress disordered from hard riding, and his boots splashed with mud up to the knees.

Him the sentries that had charge of the entrance of the tent would have forbad to go in, but he cried out with a loud voice that he must and would speak to the Lord Lieutenant, and that he came charged with urgent tidings to him from Sir Henry Harrington.

Hearing this his Excellency himself turned round, demanding to know what he had to say; whereupon the man, without speaking, thrust into his hand a small roll of paper, which was not a proper letter, but rather a wisp or loose twist of paper, as if one had snatched up the first thing that came to hand and written upon it. This my Lord took and began to read, glancing back as he did so at the messenger. But no sooner had he cast eyes upon the first words than he leaped from his seat, and the blood flew to his face in a great rush, and his eyes lit up, as do the eyes of an eagle, and—

' Fellow ! ' cried he with a loud voice, and with that made a step forward as if he would have taken him by the throat. Suddenly stopping himself—

' Where gat you that ? ' he asked, striking the paper violently with his hand as he spoke.

' From Sir Henry Harrington, my Lord ' answered the man boldly.

' You lie Sirrah ! ' shouted his Excellency furiously.

' I lie not my Lord ; he bade me make all speed, and deliver it straight into your Lordship's own hands.'

' You lie, I say ! you lie ! 'Sdeath ! it cannot be ! He dares not ! 'Fore God ! he dares not ! Defeated ! and no reason given ! Defeated, and with every advantage of ground and numbers ! Defeated ! and by a crew of ragged Irish kernes and runagates ! Fled from the field, leaving his baggage and wounded behind him ! Hell and Furies ! 'tis impossible ! 'Tis too monstrous an invention ! Speak fellow ! Some enemy hath be-

guiled this into thee. Speak I say! Confess that
'tis a lie, and I will forgive thee.'

''Tis no lie, my Lord' answered the other
sturdily. ''Tis the very Gospel truth, and I who
speak to your Lordship know it to be so. And for
those advantages of which your Lordship speaks,
had you seen as I did that Devil's Spawn of Irish
rushing out of the rocks, and falling upon our men
ere half of them knew what had chanced, or could
get their weapons ready, you had scarce said that,
no, nor marvelled that they were overtaken with
terror, seeing that they were but men, after all, and
not wizards or magicians, such as 'twould take to
cope with such a Satan's brood, the very sight and
hellish noises whereof were enough to scare any
Christian man!'

'Silence cur!' shouted his Excellency. 'What
thou white-blooded slave and traitor! art not
ashamed to stand there and openly defend such
cowardice? Ho guards, seize, bind, and carry him
away! Let none have communication with him
lest this contamination spread. As I am a Christian
'tis enough to make any one believe the very air of
this country to be bewitched, so that it exhales
treason as a marsh exhales vapours! That a man
should be found to stand up—untouched in body

and limb—and openly avow such cowardice! By my oath, if the Queen have many more of that kidney in her Irish army 'twere a plain alms to hang 'em!'

Then there was a great hasting to and fro, the Council having to be newly assembled, several of its members being dispersed, and needing to be recalled to decide what was to be done. And that night 5 companies of foot and 2 of horse were despatched in all haste to see what had in truth befallen Sir Henry Harrington, and to rally those troops which had got dispersed through the country.

His Lordship meantime with the main body moved on into the lord Poer's country, and thence to Waterford, where they camped within 3 miles of that city. But, when the messengers sent by the officer in command returned, they brought word that matters were even as the first messenger had said; nay 't was worse than he reported, many of the soldiers under Sir Henry Harrington having not only lost all discipline, but being filled with terror beyond reason, had fled madly away, tearing off their uniforms and throwing down their weapons lest they should betray them; and had hidden themselves in rocks and holes of the earth, not daring to venture out till the troops sent in search of them appeared, whereupon they gladly rendered themselves up, though knowing that they would receive the punishment of their cowardice, yet preferring to die by their comrades' hands, than to be starved to death, or fall into the hands of the rebels, of whose cruelty they stood in such exceeding dread.

Having received the reports of this matter, and commanded that those who had so dishonoured themselves and disgraced the name of soldier should be sent to Dublin, there to be kept until his return, when a Court Martial would sit upon them, his Excellency set himself to review her Majesty's magazines of victual and munition at Waterford. And this done, upon the 22nd of June, he set forth from that town, and came to Passage, a village so called because it is beside the ferry leading from the county of Waterford into the county of Wexford. Here he had commanded all the boats of Waterford, Rosse and the Carick to be gathered together to transport the army across. But because the place was very wide, the number of boats small, and the carriage far greater than had ever been seen before in this country with so few fighting men, there was great difficulty and much delay, so that by night-time only a small portion of the horse were got across.

What added no little to the difficulty was that the weather, which for a week past had been very bad, upon that day exceeded all that ever I saw for wetness, the rain coming down in torrents, so that many thought that Noah's Deluge must have come again, and much of the baggage was lost, and several of the horses killed through slipping and falling upon the wet rocks. And whether this unhappy affair of Sir Henry Harrington had daunted the spirit of the army; or whether it was from the great rain, by means of which not a man walked dry, but lived soaked to the skin from the time he set forth in the morning till he came to the camping ground at night; or from the badness of the roads, which were not in truth roads but blind tracks; or from the want of proper food, and the great difficulty of cooking it, so that the men were often forced to swallow their meat raw; or from the increasing prevalence of sickness; or whatever else the reason may have been, certain it is that from that time forth a great dissatisfaction took possession of the troops, many even who were of much higher rank than the common soldiery, scrupling not to complain; saying that they had accompanied his Excellency from England to win honour and renown, and not to be starved to death, or drowned with rain, or lost in foul and noisome bog holes, or shot by naked savages from behind rocks, and many other such-like unreasonable and unsoldierly complaints. And as straws will sometimes shew how the wind bloweth, when bulkier objects are a less good index, so I will here set down a conversation which I heard between two of the foot soldiers not far from Ballybrenan, as we were on the way to Wicklow.

That night, it being not only exceedingly wet, but also blowing a great gale of wind, it chanced that on my way to his Lordship's tent I was forced to shelter myself against a hedge, or rather a sort of thorn-grown thicket, till the violence of the storm had a little abated. And as I stood there I presently perceived that two of the sentries, whose duty it was to remain in the open, had also taken refuge from the storm upon the other side of the same thicket, and were crouched upon the ground, muttering one to another, not having observed my coming, owing to the rain and wind, which filled both their ears and their eyes.

'A murrain upon this Irish expedition!' one said to the other, 'a murrain upon it, and upon those that sent us on 't! May I be a heathen if I know what it is to have a dry rag to my back, or a bit of whole skin to my toes. Odsbodikins, man, an 't were not for this rain which would put out all the fires ever Satan lighted, I would swear we must by this time have got to the very gates of Hell, if no i' th' inside of Hell itself.'

'Aye, that would I, that would I too, Timothy Nuthatch,' muttered the other. 'The devil take Irish wars one and all, say I. What with early starts and late marches I am a garron if I have not a'most forgotten the very look o' roast meat! How many times since we set out from Dublin has my belly been so flat and pinched after an hour's walking that I ha' been fain to snatch at the filthy berries growing out of the hedge side, or to pick a sallet of green herbs as I skirted a ditch back, and what sort of food, I ask you, is a sallet of green herbs to put into the inside of a man, save to chill his stomach further this cold and colicky weather?'

'Aye, aye,' muttered the first, ''tis little they that ride at their ease care how the foot-soldier fares. And further I tell you, Bill Bradshaw, that——'

With this he sunk his voice so low that I heard

naught, only the curses that broke from them from time to time, and the grunts and groans of their complaining, more like filthy swine than men and soldiers. And the rain having somewhat abated, I passed on, thinking within myself that no amount of conduct in the commander, nor yet of courage in the better soldiery, will avail much when the main bulk of an army is made up of such soft and brabbling stuff as this, which be scarce fit to carry the munition of true warriors. And of this I soon after had a most fit proof and illustration. For only the very next day, being assailed on our road by a small party of the rebels near Eniscorthy, I saw these two fellows, Timothy Nuthatch and Bill Bradshaw run past as 't were for the bare life, their pikes flung down, their garments awry, and they themselves looking back at the Irish that followed, as if the very Arch Fiend himself with a Garrison-full of Devils were at their heels. And but for the sudden resolution of Colonel Fellowes, who— being at the time somewhat in the rear—got upon a whin-bank, and called out loudly that he would himself shoot dead the first man who passed him, thereby catching them betwixt two fires, it might readily have befallen that the alarm thus kindled, would have spread throughout the whole army.

For this sort of blind terror or panic is in truth of the very nature of a Conflagration, which being caught by one substance spreads to another, and so to the next and the next till all be consumed. Nor, when once 'tis established, does it need any real or present peril to produce it, but the veriest fancy, and image of danger—nay the harmless falling of a stone, or innocent report of a pith gun —will suffice to awaken it, when off they go, helter skelter, like a flock of sheep, swearing, crying out, falling one against another, striking, wounding, aye even pressing one another to death in their madness. So that at last they bring upon themselves that peril which at first was nothing but a sort of Conjuration, emitted by their own flat and dastardly spirits.

Upon which subject, as upon many others which this campaign has brought before my mind, I might readily here fill many pages, yet will I forbear to do so, fearing to fatigue the reader, the readier that larger and weightier matters do beckon us steadily forward into the Future.

XIV

AT a council held by his Excellency at Ennis-
corthy it was decided we should not go by the
Duffrey—which is the commonest road to Dublin
—the reason being that the ways there were
known to be all plashed, but by Fernes and
Arklow, and should march in the strongest and
swiftest order we could, seeing that these Leinster
rebels were certainly out in great force, of whom
the most important, I was told, were the Kavenaghs,
the O'Byrnes, the O'Tooles, the O'Connor Falys,
the O'Mores of Leix, with some of the lesser
traitors of Low Leinster and their bonnaghts.

The chief cause of delay, and main impediment
to our march both now and ever since we left
Dublin was the great train of churles, horse boys,
and such unserviceable people with which our
army was clogged. For the number of these '*Black
Guards*' (so called because with them travel the
cooks, with their pots, pans and other kitchen gear)

was said to be nearly a third of the whole army. Most of these were, by his Excellency's orders, left behind at Arklow, so that with a lighter running camp he might more readily attempt the rebels ; and, having passed the ford nigh to that place, he pushed on along the higher ground, the rebels, (fearing ever to be taken upon a good champion field!) keeping upon our left hand side, and somewhat nearer to the sea.

It was close to this town of Arklow that a great disaster was nigh happening through the fault of the guides, they having carried the Earl of Ormonde with the Marshal and the Vanguard along the sea shore, where, the ground being low, they could see neither the country around them nor their own wings, so that the rebels got between them and the main body. Fortunately his Excellency, having just then mounted to the top of one of the hills that stood near, perceived the rebel force, some nine hundred strong, marching to cut off our carriage and the left wing. Sending therefore to the rearward for three hundred of the lightest foot and all the horse, he, with the Earl of Southampton and others, galloped swiftly down hill to the rescue of our men, who were like to have been cut in pieces. At this the rebels, who

were just then crossing a bog, having a low wood
in front of it and sand hills in the rear, stopped
short, but seeing the small number of our men,
they came on again with great speed, uttering
the most frightful, heathenish, and soul-terrifying
noises. Whereupon the Earl of Southampton, who
was given the command of the horse, gave them a
charge so resolute and so home that he drave
them back upon the wood, and entering after them
followed them right up to the bog, by means of
which Captain Constable, Mr. Cox and some
others, who had followed too eagerly, got bogged,
and were forced to quit their horses, Mr. Cox
being badly wounded by a chance shot.

For the foot soldiers they again shewed a very
different spirit from the horse, displaying the most
shameful terror at the approach of the rebels,
crying out to one another that they were certainly
Devils, for that they could see red and fiery horns
rising up out of their heads, with other such-
like cries of amazement, most lamentable and
unsoldier-like to hear. Fortunately the rebels,
delaying for their main body to approach, gave
our horsemen from the rearward also time to come
up, who, charging boldly, drove them back across
the bog, and so up against the Earl of South-

ampton, who again repulsed them, whereupon they
fled in great disorder, many throwing away their
arms, and some getting in their turn stuck in the
bog, where they were overtaken and killed by our
men, who followed the pursuit with great diligence,
although at a disadvantage, being so much more
heavily clad and accoutered than those they were
pursuing.

The pursuit being at length over, towards four
of the clock one of the chiefs, called the O'Connor
Faly, sent a follower to his Lordship to crave
permission to speak with him about conditions.
The same came to us at Arklow, where his Excellency had just entered a house. Whom, when the
officers without perceived, they would have cut him
down. But his Lordship, hearing of his coming,
gave orders that he should be allowed to enter,
which he did, and came forward clad in the Irish
dress, with woollen trews of a striped pattern, his
bratt about his shoulders, his arms bare, wearing
a lip-beard, his forelocks long, and hanging over
his eyes in a tangled mass. A larger-bodied man
I have rarely seen, nor one of a more dour aspect,
rising over six feet in height, and standing there
(though alone, his friends newly dispersed, and
himself surrounded by so many gleaming swords

which ached to find themselves in his vitals,) with a look as haughty and a carriage as dauntless as though we had been his vassals, and he our Prince and Better.

Finding that he knew no English, an interpreter was sent for to enquire his errand, whereupon he told that this O'Connor Faly craved to speak with the Lord Lieutenant, but only on condition of a safe conduct to come and go. To which his Excellency replied that if O'Connor Faly came as a repentant rebel, without arms, offering himself in absolute submission to Her Majesty he might do so, and have a safe conduct, but that if he came in other guise or for any other purpose, he should have none, and that as for the next messenger he would be hanged. This being repeated in Irish to the man, he replied haughtily in his own tongue that O'Connor Faly would come in no such way, nor for any such purpose, and so saying turned himself round and strode resolutely out of the house. At which some of the younger captains standing by would have gone after him and cut him down, but his Excellency forbade it, and so the man got clear away.

This happened at Arklow, where my Lord lay that night, and the day following we marched to

Wicklow, and encamped three miles short of it
close to the place where Sir Henry Harrington's
disaster befel, and from thence shaped our course
direct to Dublin.

Shortly after leaving Arklow we entered a valley
very pleasing of appearance, the name of which I
was told was the Vale of Avoca, which methought
had a melodious sound, such as might fitly find
place in some sonnet or madrigal, were a poet
moved to indite one upon such a place, which I
can scarce suppose, seeing that he would prefer
to leave it to its brutish obscurity. The hills,
though high, were not so lofty as to be displeasing,
being well clothed with verdure to the top, the
woods having a park-like aspect, so that one gazing
at them and not knowing where he was, might have
said—' Sure, this is the estate of some noble Lord
or worthy Gentleman, who hath planted these fair
mounts, and laid out these woods to walk in, yea
and directed these sparkling rivulets, which fall
with so pleasant a sound over the rocks ? ' Natheless no Gentleman or Nobleman of a surety had
ought to do with it ; only Nature, who being a
woman and therefore unaccountable, will as readily
endow a region given over to godless runagates
like these O'Byrnes as one inhabited by a more

God-fearing and obedient people. For since the
first coming of the English these O'Byrnes of
Wicklow have been a sore plague and offence, so
that the whole region Stinketh in the Nostrils of all
that be sent to govern Ireland, having bred more
notable rebels than any other part, unless it be
the Kingdom, (as of the ignorant it is called) of
Kerry.

At our last halting place before entering Dublin,
his Lordship lodged in the house of one Mr.
Barker. Yet, though his quarters here were of
unwonted ease and dryness, he was much plagued
with the ague, and with darting pains in the lower
limbs, so that he could gain no sleep. Accordingly called to me, who lay near him, and desired
that I would repeat some verses, either of Edmund
Spenser or some other of our recent poets, so that
by the power of well-linked words his spirit might
be wooed to slumber.

'Alas, my Lord,' said I, 'gladly would I do so,
but, as I have oft told your Lordship, my memory
is of that defective quality that for very shame I
durst never repeat the poesy of any other man,
fearing lest his thoughts and melody suffer some
injury at my hands.'

'Repeat me then some of thine own, most

musical of Hals,' quoth he smiling, 'some sonnet or roundelay, and the cheerfuller the better ; only, as you love me, not one of those dolorous love ditties of thine, which be altogether too sorrowful for a man whose days are at best none of the cheerfullest.'

So, being set to this task (which in truth and without vanity I would have avoided) I bethought what I had that were best suited to the occasion.

'Would your Lordship,' said I, 'be pleased to hear an hunting song, which I have writ and composed not long since ? '

'An hunting song ! Why, gladly ! ' cried he, 'that were the very thing ! Some merry rousing strain, to carry my thoughts from all that oppresses them here. I knew, not, my dolorous Hal, you had any such in your wallet, and am the better pleased.'

'For mirthfulness I know not that it be greatly of that complexion, my Lord,' said I, 'but such as it is your Lordship shall hear, and judge for yourself.'

Then I began to rehearse the following verses, of which there were altogether forty-seven, but the whole I give not.

Hunting Song.

When beached streams run thick and slow,
And efts upclimb, with oosy slime,
And only marish blossoms blow,
  Then comes the merry hunting time,
  Blow ! blow ! the merry hunting time.

When all the ways are dark and brown,
And not a bird uplifts its strain,
And leaves come circling slowly down,
  Then starts the merry hunting train,
  Blow ! blow ! the merry hunting train.

When rain-drops stand on every ledge,
And, all forlorn, the forests mourn,
And daily starker grows the hedge,
  Then sounds the merry hunting horn,
  Blow ! blow ! the merry hunting horn.

When Time the gold with grey replaces,
And mocks with scorn the hues of morn,
And thins the long-remembered faces,
  Then sounds the merry hunting horn,
  Blow ! blow ! the merry hunting horn.

 . . . . . .

'Now by St. Hubert !' cried his Excellency, starting up from where he lay. 'This hunting song of thine, good Hal, is the dolefullest doleful ditty that ever yet I heard. Not another verse an you love me! So help me all good lovers of sport 'twere enough to make any one drown

himself in sheer despite, and of drowning we ha'
enough in this clime without it. Take it not un-
kindly, man, that I make short work of thy remaining verses. Some other time, when all goes
well, and our spirits, being too boisterous, need
chastisement, I will apply to thee for the remainder, but at present—Abstain, good Hal!
Abstain!'

'Verily my Lord' said I, somewhat mortified,
'I feared as much, and warned you of the same
ere I began. For, as your Lordship is aware, that
which proceeds out of a man, whether it be prose
or in poesy, is apt to be of the same complexion
as the man himself, and my thoughts of late have
been but of a dolorous hue.'

'I know it, good Hal,' said he, 'and think not
the worse of thee, rather the better. Natheless I
must pray your forgiveness for cutting short these
same mournful warblings of thine, seeing that the
listening to many more in the same strain would
in my present mood be not unlike pouring water
down the throat of a man new pulled out of a
river!'

This conversation—though pertaining rather to
the domain of private than public interest—I here
offer to the reader, not from any satisfaction which

it gives me to repeat these poor verses of mine own invention, but simply because my Lord gave me such strict charge to write down everything that befel upon our journey, the lighter matters, no less than the graver. For the same reason, and because of the closeness of my attendance on him, I find that mine own slighter concerns tend to get as it were mixed and interfused with his, so that 't is difficult for me to disentangle one from the other—although to allow such a thing savours, I know, of irreverence. Which explanation given, I would further entreat the reader's permission to record yet another conversation which took place somewhat before this time, and which I then spake not of, though it wrought in me no little trouble, and even now the remembrance lies like lead upon a soul that was none too jocund before.

It befel in this wise. It chanced that a gentleman, by name Mr. Allardice, had ridden from Dublin with letters to my Lord, and came into the camp. Whom shortly after his arrival, I, entering into conversation with him, begged to inform me of all that had befallen since our departure, which he obligingly did, relating, amongst other matters, how that the young Burke of Clanrickard—upon whose behalf I had interceded with his Excellency—had recently been released from his fetters, though still kept in custody as a matter of precaution.

'And Mistress Agatha Usher' I enquired, endeavouring to speak in careless wise, yet my heart bumping up and down the while in my breast, like some poor bird's that is caught in the hand of a fowler. 'How doth that gracious and modest maiden? I trust well, but have heard naught of her since our first setting forth.'

'For well' said Mr. Allardice, 'I doubt not she is well enough, and modest too I hope, as gentlewomen go, but Mistress Usher is she no longer, for she was married some three weeks since to young Mr. Oliver Morrison, eldest son to Sir Richard Morrison, newly made knight by his Excellency, and as I am informed, a pretty springal, of no small parts and promise. But God-a-mercy, Master Secretary! what ails you? You look as linen-cheeked as though you were about to swoon! Pray God you be not seized with this country's sickness, which is so plaguey rife this season. If so, a cup of aniseed water, with a few toasted crabs in it, is of excellent efficacy, or could you get at it, some of the right Origanum finely powdered,

with six drops of distilled Dragon's blood, is even
yet more sovereign, but that I fear is scarce
procurable in this outlandish region.'

'Nay 'tis nothing' said I, 'only a sudden
vertigo or gidyness to which I am subject from a
boy. I will but take a few turns in the air, and 't
will presently pass off.'

'Do so ; do so,' cried he, 'for indeed you look
but poorly.'

'And is it thus?' said I to myself when I
was alone. 'Is it thus, Oh thou poor weak believing Fool! that thou again findest thyself cast off,
disappointed, and left forlorn? Verily 'tis enough
for thee to set heart upon some hope, for that hope
to be forthwith quenched, darkened, and lost in the
common clouds. Was it for this, that thou and
that False Fair One did hold together such sweet
and harmonious discourse? For this that thou
nursed her image within thy breast, ever turning
to it as to a ray of sunshine in a dark and lonesome
land? For this that thy heart hath so leaped ever
since thy steps have begun to turn Dublin-wards?
Go to, Fool, and know that Woman is, and hath
been from the beginning of time but a rainbow,
and a twinkling delusion, ever beckoning on a man
with soft words and softer looks, till—her purpose

being gained—she leave him but the darker and the more blinded for her deceitfulness.'

And, my thoughts being thus worked upon, began presently to resolve themselves into the fashion of a sonnet, which sonnet I insert, not, I would again assure the reader, from any uneasy vanity, (that being, as all are aware, at no time a malady of mine) but because when a man is truly and by his constitution a Poet, then poesy—being the natural fruit of his soul—giveth a livelier image of his thoughts than can hope to be compassed by him in plain prose. And this sonnet ran as follows.

To a False and Fickle Fair

As morning mists, with tender blandishment,
Kiss some sad hill upon its sad cold brow,
Then, melting off with slow evanishment,
Leave what was barren erst more barren now.
As thin-veined leaves, led on by odorous May,
O'er some bare trunk a flickering verdure shed,
Then, wooed by boisterous Autumn, slip away
Leaving its bareness yet more sere and dead.
As Ocean waves, a frolic company,
With leap on leap cover the cold brown sands,
Then with one huddling impulse seaward flee,
And what was naked erst more naked stands.
So to my grief-filled heart False Fair art thou,
And what was GLOOM before, is THRICE GLOOM now!

And, being thus poetically delivered, my soul

felt somewhat easier. For poetry has in it of the nature of a Cataplasm, or Poultice, which, when laid upon a sore place sucketh from it its worst poison, and leaveth it less like to cause mortification. Yet was I still beset with many grievous thoughts, so that with sundry sighs and not a few salt tears I ruefully watered the road to Dublin, in which town it was no little solace to me to find that my Lord purposed taking up his residence in the Castle, and not in the house of Mr. Usher, the very sight of which house would have been to me as is the sight of some chalice or goblet—no matter how finely it may be gilt—to one who has drunk from it some Nauseous Draught, the remembrance of which still clings like the flavour of bitter aloes about his lips.

XV

HARDLY had he set foot in Dublin than my Lord was forced to surrender himself into the charge of the physicians, in whose hands he lay several days, suffering many things of them both internally and externally ; which doings, if they relieved him little, (nay, so far as I could observe, increased his maladies) gave at least great satisfaction to those gentlemen, he being the First in this land, and they at that time somewhat scant of patients.

While still beholden to them for these services he was likewise forced (so great was the pressure upon his time) to receive and answer a number of letters from all parts of Ireland, as well as to entertain many suitors, which he did, lying in his bed, and endeavouring as best he could in that position, to give them both his attention and their satisfaction.

Nor were these the worst of the burdens laid upon him, for it was at this time that letters

P

began to reach him in large numbers both from her
Majesty and the English Council, touching events
recently befallen; which letters, (I say it in all
reverence for the greatness of their writers!) were
not of a nature either to calm or to hearten a sick
man; especially one to whom the voice of reproof
has been from childhood as is the touch of a spur
to the flanks of a gallant but over mettlesome steed.

For of all those who in times past had declared
their love for my Lord, there were at this time as
I understood but three whose affection could be
relied upon, namely,—The Lord Keeper Egerton,
the most Reverent Archbishop John Whitgift, and
his Lordship's uncle, good Sir William Knollys
the Comptroller, who of late they say rarely
attendeth Council. For the rest, their great aim
seemed how best to thwart my Lord, and most to
mis-report and represent his actions, so that whatever he did, that, in their opinion was the thing
he ought not to have done.

Thus on the occasion of the Court Martial
held upon the officers and soldiers under Sir Henry
Harrington, my Lord had decided that with regard
to that knight himself—he being a member of the
Irish Council—he should not be brought to judgment till the Queen's pleasure about him should be

known. For the common soldiers it was at first proposed that of those clearly proved to have shown cowardice the whole should be put to death, a punishment which my Lord of his own motion and pity afterwards reduced, commanding that they should cast dice amongst themselves, and that only one in ten, he upon whom the lot fell, should be executed.

So accordingly it was done, those upon whom the lot fell being shot, the rest standing by and being returned to prison after the execution was over. Now this—though clearly a mitigation and tenderness—was, I heard, loudly cried out against by the Queen's Council ; nay the very Pick-thanks and common Newsmongers, (of which these idle times see so many) complained against it, scrupling not to say that my Lord did it to cause terror, and to exalt his own office, wishing to king it over here in Ireland. So that, as he himself said, he was required to be at once Lord Authority, and Lord Mockery, a seeming solid substance, but in reality only hung out in these Irish wastes as a Puppet of the State, as men hang mawkins in beanfields, which, though without arms or legs, yet, being blown about by the wind, seem at a distance to move and to be endowed with life.

In the same way it is, I hear, loudly complained of in England that his Excellency has given away too much of the confiscated lands, and been over free also with the honour of knighthood. Yet we who are upon the spot know that such complaints are but as the sighing of a summer breeze in comparison to the loud outcries made in Ireland by those who have expected such rewards but received none. Especially those that would possess themselves of the confiscated lands being so vehement and clamorous in their supplications that my Lord at this time could scarce ride along the streets of Dublin for the noise of their importunities. And more than once he complained of the same in my hearing, nor was I surprised, such covetousness being so contrary to his own nature that he could scarce credit it in others.

'Pardieu! I wonder what would they have?' cried he. 'Do they wish me to cut up my own body into pieces for them? Can I—that am but one man, and a subject to boot—carve out kingdoms, lordships, counties, large and fertile estates and properties, and all that such a crew of leeches may batten and grow fat upon them at their pleasure? Have the gluttons never bethought them that they are men, and must die therefore,

like their betters? 'Fore God! one would almost
believe that they alone were to cheat Sir Worm,
and batten till the day of Doom upon the lands of
other, and perchance not so very much worse men!
Not a parcel of land, not a patch of bog, not so
much as a paltry sheep-walk going in this country
but fifty of these land-beggars, who would elsewhere be earning their own livelihood, clamour
after it, yelping and hoiting like a pack of hounds,
or like those many-legged vermin the caterpillar-
worms, that thirst to get hold of some goodly
garment, though when they have it they use it for
no better purpose but to stuff out their own hollow
insides with it.'

'Faith, my Lord,' I answered on that occasion,
'I remember to have heard it said, or seen it writ
somewhere, that no roaring lion is so savage or
clamorous as an hungry office-seeker or petitioner
when he is baulked of his prey.'

'A lion, Hal! wrong not the poor beast by any
such comparison!' cried he, 'Vermin! Vermin, I
call them! and ugly crawling vermin to boot! I
swear to you since I have been in Ireland I have
met with but one man who has not straightway
begged some post or some piece of land from
me, and that man was Sir Conyers Clifford.'

'That, my Lord' said I, 'I can well believe. Nor are there many that in my humble opinion can compare with Sir Conyers, both for generosity of nature or for conduct when in the field. Hath your Lordship, I pray you, heard lately from that good knight, for meseems 'tis a long time since he was last reported of.'

'I do expect to hear of him hourly' replied his Excellency. 'And at present as I understand he should be to the north of the county of Mayo, and by the first or second of next month, I look to him to join me at the Navan, there to aid in the assembling of the forces which are to take the field against Tyrone.'

This conversation, as I but too clearly recall, befell upon a Thursday, and the very next day but one, being a Saturday, I was writing in the ante-room to the presence chamber, when I heard my Lord coming hastily up the stairs, and, looking round, saw a terrible look upon his face, which told me without questioning that some new and perchance more direful disaster had befallen.

And the minute he caught sight of me he cried with a loud voice, 'Hal, Hal! Sir Conyers Clifford is slain!'

'For the love of God, my Lord, say not

so !' exclaimed I, leaping to my feet. 'Sure how can that be ? Hath he already encountered Tyrone, and the other chief enemies from the North ?'

'No Hal, he hath been slain at a place called the Curlews in Mayo by a crew of O'Rourkes and O'Donnells, and all that were with him are put to flight or slaughtered, and Sir Alexander Ratcliffe is also dead, and the rebels have possession of the bodies of them both !'

Then I was the more troubled, knowing how the heads and limbs of rebels are set up in all public places in Ireland, and fearing greatly that when they in their turn had got possession of the bodies of two such honourable gentlemen as Sir Conyers Clifford and Sir Alexander Ratcliffe they would assuredly work despite upon their remains, if only in revenge of the like dealing. In this, however, twas after found that the rascals showed a better spirit than might have been expected, for they disposed of them both fittingly, giving them honourable burial in a Christian churchyard, as we were informed.

But my Lord strode to and fro the room, as his wont is when disturbed. And every minute he broke into fresh anger and fresh lamentations, clenching his hands, and striking upon the ground with his foot.

' The Curlews ! ' cried he, ' What in God's name is the Curlews ?   Who ever heard of the Curlews ? Is that a place for a knight of fame and daring to be overthrown and slain ? Some demon sure must overhang this land and all that come into it, else 't could never arrive that a noble knight and an accomplished captain should be overcome by a crew of rogues, and halter-sacks, without for the most part shoe to foot, coat to back, or knowledge and understanding of arms ! '

Then—pausing suddenly in his going—he smote his two hands together, crying out ' Death and the Devil ! now too, when every man that can put foot to ground, or leg in stirrup must be gathered together for this Northern enterprise.   Were it not for that assuredly I would go myself and avenge him.   Aye, would I, Sir Conyers, and as God is my witness I would wreak a right bloody revenge for this your slaying ! '

Hearing him so speak, I too felt that, (little of a warrior as I am by profession) I had gladly myself taken sword and shield for the avenging of that good knight, the remembrance of whose kindness to me and to my dear lad Francis

Gardner, was like a two-edged dart in my side, so that but for shame I might have played the woman, so it irked me to think of him lying there, dead, cold, and unshriven in a savage land, and 'mid fierce and wolfish foes.

What more even than his death itself troubled me, and what I could not forbear reflecting upon was that this second disaster, coming, as it did, so close upon the great scandal and disgrace of Sir Henry Harrington's defeat in Wicklow, would surely work my Lord sore harm, he having so many enemies, and they so loud and clamorous against him. But of this he himself seemingly thought little, though in all the years I have known him, and of all the deaths, both through sickness and in the tented field with which his path hath been beset, I have never known him so afflicted by any death as by this one, so that for several nights after this he would even in his sleep start up suddenly, crying out the name of Sir Conyers, and of that woeful place the Curlews, and of all there befel.

This going on some time, I being witness of his affliction, began to fear that it might work in him some lasting injury. As indeed it probably would have done, but that in this land of Ireland [however few its other merits] this one clear and absolute advantage must be admitted to it, which is that no man will ever have time to grow very sick or desperate there upon a single Trouble, seeing that in a brief space of time he may be quite sure that it will be overtaken and driven from his mind by some other and yet Worse One, ever following close after it, and treading hard upon its heels!

XVI

BY what evil enchantment it befel that having at
the onset as 't was said numbered nearly nineteen
thousand men both of horse and foot, the army
under his Excellency had by this time so dwindled
—what with sickness, losses in the field, the sup-
plying of garrisons, and such like causes—as scarce
to reckon four thousand, and that too after fresh
reinforcements had been sent from England—I,
being no soldier, dare not declare. Enough that
't was so, and, being so reduced, and the new levies
so poor in quality, and the recent terror of a
Spanish Landing so fresh in all men's minds, it
was openly said of many in the Irish Council that
't were better not to attempt any Northern enterprise this season, but remaining in Dublin, have
all in readiness to take the field early upon the
ensuing spring.

That to this counsel his Excellency would
give no ear all who know him will believe. And

although, through the defection of many, and through that ill hap which like some envious influence has dogged his steps ever since he set foot in Ireland, it was scarce to be hoped that any great advantage would be obtained, still, even to confront the Arch traitor, and oblige him to recognise some Power greater than his own frowardness and insolence, were in itself clearly no light or unworthy enterprise.

This being decided upon, and the Rendezvous, as 't is called, of the army being appointed to be at the Navan, upon the 28th day of August his Excellency rode out from Dublin, and, taking with him an escort of an hundred horse, slept that night at Ardbrackan, an house of the lord Bishop of Meath.

Next day he met the whole army upon the hill of Clythe, which is about half a mile from Kells, and the night following encamped at Castle Keran, where he was forced to remain till the victuals from Dredagh [1] overtook him. These having at last arrived he marched the army towards Fermoy, and lodged it between Robertstown and Newcastle, and the following day, the 3rd of September, moved thence to Ardee, where for

Drogheda.

the first time we came within sight of Tyrone,
he being camped out here with all his forces upon
a hill about a mile and a half from our quarters,
having only a river and wood between him and us.

Now so soon as 't was reported of the Avaunt
guard that Tyrone was within sight, immediately
there ran through the whole army a great stir,
buzz, and commotion, this Arch-traitor having been
the mark at which our aim had been set ever since
his Excellency first came to Ireland, and he being
so much spoken of, yet hitherto seen of but few,
and they not recently. His Excellency was himself more eager to meet him than was the youngest
man under arms, so hastened the troops forward,
and embattled them that day in force upon the hill
by the burnt castle of Ardee. Finding that there
was no wood for firing save in the valleys towards
Tyrone's quarter, he presently commanded that a
squadron from each company should go out and
fetch it in, and sent 500 foot and 2 companies of
horse to be their guard ; whereupon Tyrone sent
out some of his men to offer battle, but after a
while directed them not to pass the ford, ours being
so resolved to dispute it. At this first meeting
some slight skirmishing took place from one side
of the river to the other, but to no great purpose,

for as they offended us little, so we troubled ourselves little about them.

Next day we marched through the plain country
to the mill of Louthe, and encamped beyond the
river, Tyrone also marching through the woods
and keeping his scouts of horse well in sight of our
quarter. Here we were forced to delay again for
a fresh supply of victuals from Dredagh, upon
which his Excellency, (whom this new delay fretted
not a little) summoned a Council of War to consider what was to be done upon Tyrone's army.
Of this Council the greater number were more
than ever of opinion that 'twas impossible to fight
upon such disadvantage ; our army being both fewer
in number, they said, and worst posted ; an opinion
at which his Excellency chafed violently, it being
as Wormwood to his spirit that he should be within
sight of Tyrone, yet hindered still from fighting
him.

Upon the afternoon of the same day between
the hours of four and five of the clock, there
came riding towards us out of the camp of the
rebels three men, all well mounted and accoutered.
And the midmost man carried at the end of his
riding rod a white scarf, in token that he was the
bearer of a message, and craved a Safe conduct.

When his Lordship, who was at the door of his tent, saw these three draw near, he called quickly for his horse, and, desiring us that were about him to follow, he rode forward a little way, and waited for them to draw near.

Then the midmost man, who was clearly also chief of the three, so soon as he had come near my Lord, made an humble obeisance, doffing his hat down to the ground ; his Lordship barely touching his own hat, and looking sternly at him the while. And when he was within speaking distance,

'Who are you, sir?' asked his Excellency, 'And for what purpose come you before our host ?'

'I come, my Lord' said the other, louting again, yet speaking in a clear loud voice, 'from the most noble Earl of Tyrone, who craves speech with your Lordship, and would have you admit him to parley, seeing that he has that to say which concerns your private ear.'

'For speech, sir' said my Lord, 'methinks 't were time enough for that when the Earl of Tyrone lays by his arms, and craves her Majesty's mercy. But who are you I say? for by your speech you are, I take it, no Irishman.'

'Nor am I my Lord, and for my name it is

Hubert Walters, formerly in one of her Majesty's troop of horse, but for these last five years in the service of the Earl of Tyrone. And this I say openly, and in the hearing of yonder gentlemen, that her Majesty hath had no more faithful servant than that noble Earl, nor would ever have had but that the craft of evil speakers, seeking their own ends, gat between him and her Grace, and so forced him to take up arms in his own behoof, which else I, who know him intimately, can swear he would never in all the years of his life so much as have thought of.'

'You have a well-oiled tongue sir' returned his Excellency, 'an' it seems to me that the Earl of Tyrone has in you one who knows better how to set forth his cause in cunning colours than he does himself.'

'No cunning colours, my Lord' said the other, 'but simple truth and fair dealing, as your Lordship would allow were you pleased to hold parley with the Earl, and hear what he has to say in his own behoof.'

'Enough sir,' replied his Excellency turning sharply away. 'For yourself we grant you leave to retire in safety as you came. For the Earl, your master, tell him from me that he knows what is required of him, and that less will by no means serve. And that for parleying with myself, he will find me tomorrow morning upon the hill between our two camps, at the head of her Majesty's forces, where he can readily hold as much parley with me as his soul hath stomach for.'

With these words he turned away, and that Hubert Walters, with the two others; (one whom I found was called Hagan or O'Hagan, a man much favoured of Tyrone, the other, one Con O'Neale, a base-born son of his own), rode back whence they came, having gained nothing by their embassy; whereat I rejoiced not a little, having feared his Lordship might be drawn by their guile into some sudden rashness.

Next day, the 6th of September, leaving a colonel with 500 foot and 20 horse to guard our quarters and baggage, his Excellency drew out 2000 foot and 300 horse, and embattled them upon the first great hill in sight of Tyrone, then marched forward to another hill, upon which Tyrone's guard of horse stood, which no sooner saw us approach than they quitted it, and our army made good the place till near three of the o'clock, during which time Tyrone's foot never showed themselves out of the wood, while his horsemen were put from

Q

all the hills between us and the main body ; on which occasion some slight skirmishing took place amongst the light horse, in which a French gentleman of the Lord Lieutenant's troop, and an English gentleman of the Earl of Southampton's were all that were hurt on our side.

After this a horseman of Tyrone's called on us and delivered the following message ; that Tyrone would not fight nor draw forth, but desired to speak with the Lord Lieutenant, only not between the two armies. Whereupon his Excellency drew back to his quarter, and after his return placed a garrison of 500 foot and 50 horse at Niselrathy, where there was a square castle, and a great bawne with a good ditch round it, and thatched houses for our men to lodge in.

Upon the 7th we marched to Drumcondra, but ere we had got a mile on the road, Hubert Walters and Henry Hagan came again, and in the presence of the Earl of Southampton, Sir George Bourchier, Sir Warham St. Leger and other gentlemen, delivered a fresh message from Tyrone, praying her Majesty's mercy, and desiring that the Lord Lieutenant would hear him, which, if his Lordship would agree to do, he would gallop about, they said, to the ford of Bellaclinthe, which

is on the right hand side of the way to Drumcondra.

'What say you, gentlemen?' said his Lordship, turning to those about him. 'Shall we listen
to this petitioner, seeing that this is the third time
he entreats to be heard in his own behalf?'

Then the Earl of Southampton and the rest
agreeing that it were well to hear what he had to
say, his Excellency despatched two gentlemen with
Hubert Walters and Henry Hagan to view this
ford of Bellaclinthe. But when they were come
to the place they found Tyrone already there, and
the water exceeding deep, so that it seemed to
them to be no fit place to speak in. Which, they
declaring, he grew very impatient, and cried with
a loud voice—'Shall I despair then ever to speak
with him?' And, (knowing the ford) he presently
found out a place where by standing up to his
horse's belly in the water he might be near
enough to the other shore to be heard by the Lord
Lieutenant, although the latter kept to the hard
ground.

Meanwhile his Lordship, followed by the Earl
of Southampton, Sir Warham St. Leger and the
rest, and by a troop of horse, had ridden along the
summit of the hill. And, coming presently to a

halt immediately above the place, he saw Tyrone standing there alone in the water, yet doubted at first whether it was Tyrone or no.

So—turning to one that rode nearest to him— 'Tell me, I pray you,' said he, 'is that man whom I see there by himself in the water the Earl of Tyrone?' To which the other replying that it was, his Lordship suddenly exclaimed—'Then by the honour of my name, if he comes out thus alone and without fear to meet me I will not be behind him in courage or courtesy, but will also go down alone to meet him! Tarry here, Gentlemen, till my return.'

So saying, before any one could utter a word, or knew a'most what was in his mind to do, he had set spurs to his horse, and galloped down the hill towards where Tyrone was standing up to his horse's belly in the water.

When I saw that, and perceived that his Lordship had in very deed gone down alone and unguarded to meet Tyrone, I was filled with dismay, perceiving plainly that this—though done but in a sudden heat of courage and nobility— might with ease be turned to dangerous uses, and made to bear a very evil sound in the hearing of her Majesty and of the Council.

But we, standing upon that hill-side, saw Tyrone doff his hat so that it all but touched the water running below him, saluting my Lord with much humility, his Excellency at the same time riding forward a little way into the stream, so that presently they came together, and were able to speak without hindrance ; Tyrone, as was plain to be seen, urging something with great vehemence and many words ; his Lordship on the other hand maintaining a somewhat cold and reserved aspect. And so they continued together for close upon the space of half an hour, we standing above the while, and looking down with no little wonderment at this which had so suddenly befallen before our eyes. And, when they had made an end of speaking, his Lordship rode back to us, and Tyrone also rejoined his own company, which were waiting for him upon the further side.

Not many minutes after, Tyrone sent again that base-born son of his, Con O'Neil, who besought his Excellency from his father that he would let him bring down some of his principal men, and that he would also appoint a like number to come down upon the other side. To this his Lordship agreed and desired him to bring six men, which he did, namely Cormack O'Neil, McGennis, Maguire,

Ever McCowley, Hubert Walters, and one Qwyn
that came from Spain, but is an Irishman by birth.
These six with Tyrone rode down to the ford,
his Excellency also going down again to the same
place, only this time accompanied by the Earl of
Southampton, Sir George Bourchier, Sir Warham
St. Leger, Sir Henry Danvers, Sir Edward Wing-
field and myself, Henry Harvey his secretary.

At this second meeting, Tyrone and all his
company stood up to their horses' bellies in the
water, the Lord Lieutenant with his following
standing the while upon the hard ground. And
Tyrone spake a long while bare-headed, saluting
with great respect, not alone his Excellency, but all
we that came with him. After half an hour's
conference it was concluded that there should be
a meeting of commissioners next morning at a ford
near to Garrett Fleminge's castle. And so we
parted, the Lord Lieutenant marching on with
his army to Drumcondra, and Tyrone returning to
his camp.

Next day accordingly Sir Warham St. Leger,
Sir William Constable, and Sir William Warren
were sent with instructions to the place of meeting,
Tyrone, before going to parley, sending into Garrett
Fleminge's castle four of his principal men as

pledges for the safety of the commissioners. At this parley a cessation of arms was concluded for six weeks, to be continued on till May Day, or broken upon 14 days warning. It was also covenanted that any of Tyrone's confederates who would not assent to this cessation of arms should be left by him to be prosecuted by the Lord Lieutenant; that restitution should be made for all spoils within 20 days, and that for performance of the covenants the Lord Lieutenant should give his *word*, and Tyrone his *oath*.

The above covenant—which was concluded upon the 8th day of September in this our year of Grace 1599—I have been careful to set down in the exact words of the commissioners, seeing that so great a commotion has arisen over it, and that many lying buzzes are at this moment, I hear, current in England on the matter, to the great disadvantage of his Excellency, and the still greater joy of his enemies.

The matter being thus settled, Tyrone retired with all his following into the heart of his country, while his Lordship, having sent messengers with the news of the cessation to her Majesty marched to Dredagh, where he abode ten days. At the end of which time, learning that Tyrone had for a certainty retired, and being anxious to survey the country more nearly, he returned to Garrett Fleminge's castle, bringing with him his own immediate following and three companies of horse **as a guard.**

This castle stands on the left bank of the river Lagan, not far from the ford of Bellaclinthe, having a wide prospect over all the country round about, also a small stream of great clearness running through rocks at the base, and upon the north side an ancient wood of fir trees which shelters it somewhat from the violence of the blasts. Upon our first arrival the castle was very damp, the walls streaming with moisture, and having what looked to be long candles depending from every coign of masonry, and much I feared that in such sorry quarters his Excellency would be assailed anew by that ague from which he had already suffered so grievously. The soldiers, however, being sent out to bring in wood, presently built up such a fire that the light spread, not only over the whole castle, but as the night grew darker, to the very trees without, so that their trunks shone red and glowing in the darkness.

My Lord—who was of more cheerful humour that night than I had seen him for many weeks past—remained seated awhile beside the fire, now and then lifting his head and looking towards the doorway, as if expecting something that was to reach him from thence. Indeed it being already the twelfth night since the despatch of the messengers with news of the treaty with Tyrone, I knew that he looked for their return, nor wondered that the expectation should move him to some uneasiness, nay, was not a little troubled myself, fearing that the news of the said treaty would prove anything but a toothsome morsel to her Majesty's palate; she having looked for nothing less than the total defeat of Tyrone and all his following.

' May a Plain man ask of what your Discretion is thinking, that you look so solemn and owl-like ? ' his Excellency suddenly enquired, looking at me across the fire, with a whimsical and mocking smile upon his face.

' Faith my Lord,' said I, ' it seems to me that the times demand some little gravity, not only from those set on high like your Lordship, but even from those who, like myself, but share their toils ; though belike it savours of presumption in me to say so.'

' Now may the Devil, who is the begetter of all hypocrisy, take thy humility Hal ! ' cried he impatiently, 'and for the rest of thine observation, let me tell thee that my soul has not this long time back,—no, not since my first coming to Ireland— sat so lightly in my bosom as it sits to-night. Methinks I could leap and whoop as the schoolboys do when they see their holiday-time draw near; nay, I am myself a very schoolboy, who sees the end of his durance approaching? For this, I tell thee Hal, (though as yet 'tis but for thy private ear), so soon as ever these messengers sent return, and certain necessary dispositions are made —which, with God's help, will not take many days, —that very hour do I intend to mount horse, ply spur, and set sail from these shores. And then sing Ho! Hal, sing Ho for merry England! And by my faith, if they find me returning to take up again the thankless rule of this brutish country, to be styed amongst its barren bogs, and pestered by its no less barren politics, they may call Essex a Fool first, and a Meekling secondly, and that last is a name which methinks his worst enemies have never hitherto given him!'

'Yet surely my Lord,' said I, 'this office of Lord Lieutenant of Ireland is a very high and lofty one, much coveted of those that stand foremost in her Majesty's favour?'

' A high office, Hal?' cried he. 'For my part I call it a dog's office, a jade's office, an office to make a good man bad, and an indifferent man a monster! There breathes not, I believe, upon earth at this moment that man whose virtue or prudence could carry him in safety through its intricacies. Nay, 'tis my assured conviction, and I say it in all reverence, that were the Most High to despatch one of His own angelic ministers to be the Vice-regent of this distracted land, neither Gabriel nor yet Michael would return to Heaven save with a very diminished reputation, and the renown of a *Most Indifferent Administrator !* '

' Certes my Lord' said I, 'how comes it then I wonder that so many great lords should struggle and contend one with another to be the holders of so little to be desired a post?'

' You may well wonder, Sir Wisdom, nor is there any explanation that I know of, save that man, being the thing he is, ever covets what when he has got he can make least use of, and which is most like to bring him to shame and harm. But this, I tell you plainly, had I but known the half, aye or the quarter of what I know now, I had been hanged as high as Haman ere I accepted this your most lofty office of Lord Lieutenant of

Ireland.   For the man who undertakes to hold it
must be pitiless as Nero, yet must no trace of
blood be found on his hands.   He must give ear to
all petitioners, and promise to redress all wrongs,
yet must he do nothing, and perform nothing, for
that were to bring upon himself the reproach of
highmindedness.   He must know every wound and
bleeding sore with which this wretched country
bleeds to death, yet must be content to staunch
none of them, for that were costly, and money is
of all things that which her Majesty least loves to
see shed in Ireland.   He must hear everything ;
bear everything ; soothe everyone ; speak fair to
all men ; possess his soul in silence ; toil early
and late ; expend the whole of his own poor substance without hope of compensation ; compass
impossibilities ; and at the last ?——'

'At the last ? my Lord ?' I asked, seeing that
he paused.

'At the last Hal, he must expect to return to
England to be impeached there for a common
rogue and traitor !'

'Nay, my Lord !' cried I, 'Nay nay ! your
Lordship surely monsters this matter, seeing that
all who have borne rule in Ireland have not
certainly come to so tragical an end !'

'Name them then Hal! name them I say!
Take—since 'tis well to avoid too recent an instance—Sir Henry Sidney—Philip's father—was
ever better administrator, bolder captain, wiser
governor ; nobler gentleman ? and how did he end ?
No need to rehearse that end, seeing that 'tis
current and familiar to all men.   For the rest, do
you give me a list of those who have filled this
office, and I in turn will give you a list of men
who have had their hearts broken, their purses
emptied, and themselves defrauded in the end, of
all honour, joy, comfort, recompense! But enough!
The night deepens, and these—as by your uneasy
sidelong looks I perceive you think—are perilous
topics, unsafe to bestow even upon the keeping
of yonder solid-seeming walls, which, like other
walls in this country, have no doubt chinks in
them, and ears too behind those chinks belike,
for aught a man can tell to the contrary! To
bed then, Sir Wisdom, to bed, and let the jade
Care go sleep with the politicians! Henceforth—
one little swift-passing month safely over—Essex
will have naught to say to her, but will let his
beard grow in its own fashion ; speak his mind as
he listeth ; love his friends ; hate his enemies ; call
no man honest when he knows him to be a liar ;

spend his money upon his own concerns, and when
Death comes, die either peaceably in his own halls,
or else merrily in the field, not baited to death like
a foolish bull by a pack of yelping dogs, which,
though separately nought, yet suffice—being many
and he one—to break the heart and to subdue the
courage of a bolder and a less currish-natured
beast than themselves. And now again To Bed !
and sweet sleep lie upon both our eyelids, seeing
that we must be bustling and astir betimes in the
morning.'

XVII

NEXT day by six of the clock his Lordship was in the saddle, and, taking only a small guard, whom he desired to ride at some little distance in the rear, he set forth to survey the country, beginning upon the further shores of the river Lagan.

That morning, until the hour of ten or perchance eleven, the weather, I remember, was of a most unusual clearness, the distant hills being all of a fine violet hue, exceeding fair to look on, the nearer ones green, but so vivid that it was more like precious stones laid amongst the rocks than common grass and herbs. The air too was very sweet and soft, feeling like milk as it touched the cheeks, and there were many larks singing in the sky, and the clouds had a shape and a majesticalness such as I have rarely observed, seeming to float along like gallions laden with all manner of precious things, and bearing within them the messages of a great king.

My Lord was still in that same joyous temper
I had remarked in him over night, and as he rode
he seemed to drink in new gladness out of the
very air he breathed. And we two riding side by
side he discoursed to me of all that he purposed
doing upon his return to England, and of the great
joy he should feel in ridding himself of this uneasy
governance of Ireland, and of the many faithful
and loving friends he looked to meet, above all of
his dear wife, my lady the Countess, who waited so
dutifully for him at his manor house of Chartley.
Yet once I remember, he paused suddenly upon
the brink of a small green hill, as we were riding
northward, and looked round him earnestly for the
space of some five or six minutes, as if seeking
something. And at last, with a sigh—

' 'Tis an odd thought to come into a man's mind,
and why it should visit me now I know not
Hal' said he, ' but know you that had I been born
in this Land of Ireland I believe that I could have
loved it well enough, for all the trouble it has been
to me and seems like yet to be.'

' So could not I, my Lord ' I replied boldly, ' I
see nought to love in it, nor yet in its people.
And if I must speak plainly—seeing that your
Lordship twitted me only yesternight with hypocrisy

—I cannot but grudge that the rebels of this Province should have escaped as easily as they have done, and not have suffered defeat in at least one pitched battle, so as to bring them to reason, and punish them for their contumacy.'

'Thou pratest, Hal, of what thou knowest naught!' said his Lordship sharply. 'No pitched battle, Sir Ignorance, no nor twenty pitched battles would have availed aught, else, trust me, I would have tried it. There exists but one weapon would avail here, and that is a slow one to use, and an ugly one moreover to watch when in operation.'

'And that weapon, my Lord—?' I asked.

'Is Famine, Hal, Famine! Famine with the gristly face, the clattering bones, the hollow eye sockets! Famine which eats up, not the fighting men alone, but the women and the children too, till there be not one of them left.'

'Verily, my Lord' replied I, 'seeing that they be one and all either rebels themselves, or at the least kin to rebels, they seem in my humble opinion to have deserved no less.'

'And "Verily, my Lord!"' repeated he mockingly, 'for a soft-spoken poet thou art, it seems to me, about as bloody-minded a man as I have

R

often encountered. Did'st ever see a dog starve, that thou pratest of starvation so glibly ? '

' Aye, have I, my Lord, and men and women too ' I answered with some heat. ' Does not your Lordship recal the siege of St. Croix in France, and the looks of those in the street as we rode afterwards through the town ? Methinks if ever starvation were written in human lineaments 'twere written there, large and plain for all men to read.'

' Well do I recal it, Hal, and for that very reason, perchance, have I no pressing desire to renew the sight, especially in a case where I myself would be the main begetter of the same. That 'twill have to be done I doubt not, only—being but a plain man and rough soldier, not a soft-spoken Poet like thyself and the gentle Raleigh—I had as lief another undertook the office, and so spared me the execution of it. But a truce to these babblings ! Spur thy horse, man, spur it briskly, or, beshrew me we shall be benighted ere my day's round is half accomplished.'

With that we rode on rapidly, keeping at first due Northward, afterwards taking a somewhat Westerly direction, so as to attain another ford, which a fellow of the country, who had been brought as guide, undertook to shew. And as we

rode, the weather; which at first had been so prosperous, changed ; the sky getting overcast, so that
the distant hills were quite lost to sight; the wind
too rising with a moaning sound, like the murmur-
ing of many men at a distance. And towards
three in the afternoon when we had begun to go
homewards, it got yet darker, the whole floor of
heaven becoming coated with clouds ; the rain too
beginning to fall, so that we could scarce see six
perches ahead of us ; the horses stumbling, and
we being forced to move slowly because of the
roughness of the ground.

Perceiving this, his Lordship called a halt, and
commanded that the horse upon which the guide
had been set, and which bore also a soldier to
guard him, should go first, himself and I following ;
the rest to come after us two by two, keeping
closely in the same track ; it being narrow, and the
weather so thick and untoward that were any to
stray, some accident might befall. In this manner
we proceeded for about an hour, when we again
began to draw near to the river Lagan, and could
see it below us, yet so darkly that its banks were
scarce discernible from the water which ran
between them.

And now a strange and a very terrible thing

happened! For when the horse that carried the guide and soldier approached the edge, it started violently, and could by no means be induced to enter the water ; seeing which his Lordship himself rode forward, and would have made his horse enter, but it also turned back, rearing and plunging, so that it was some minutes before he could master it again. Afterwards I came to the spot, and turned myself about, in order if possible to see what it was that had so scared the horses. And lo ! a woman of great age, clad seemingly in stone grey from head to foot, was sitting upon the brink, close to the head of the ford, and staring silently down into the water. And—looking closely at her, wondering within myself what she could be doing there at that hour—I perceived that she was engaged in what appeared to be washing clothes, or some such work, and so intent was she upon this business that she never once turned her head, for all the noise and commotion that the men and horses were making about her.

'Surely' said I to myself 'this is a very strange sight ? How comes it that a woman of this great age should be sitting here alone at this hour of the evening, when throughout the whole of the day that is past we have not met with so much as one human creature, neither man nor yet woman?'

As I so thought all at once, I know not why, there leaped into my mind the remembrance of a tale told me by Mr. Delahide in Wexford, to which at the time I paid scant attention, and that he called the tale of 'THE GREY WASHER BY THE FORD.' Which tale ran that in the days of the early heathen chiefs of Ireland—about which these ignorant people boast so many vain things —whenever a great chief went out to fight in some battle from which he was not destined to come home alive, there met him at the last stream or river he had to cross a woman clad in grey, of a great age, with a face so strange of aspect, and so foully livid in colour, that it made the blood run cold simply to look at her. And this woman, said Mr. Delahide, seemed ever engaged in washing or scouring clothes, only, when the chief drew near, she, laughing horribly, would plunge her arm into the water, and hold up to him what seemed to be the phantom or image of a Dead Man. And he who looked at it knew it for a very certainty as his own semblance and counterpart, and whatever were the wounds that phantom bore—whether of the scalp, or the breast, or whatever other part of the body—those for a certainty would be the wounds of which that chief himself would die in the battle that was shortly to be fought.

Now when the recollection of that tale came back upon my mind suddenly the sight of that withered crone, which before had been but strange, became so terrible to me that my hair began to rise erect upon my head for horror, and I could scarce keep in the saddle for the shaking of all my members. And, looking round to see if any other of the party had observed her, I could not discern that any had, saving only the Irish kerne who had come with us as a guide, whose eyes, I saw, were fixed upon her, and his mouth agape with terror, yet a sort of joy breathed too, I thought, in his face, as if he knew that she had come to predict evil, not to him, but to those whom he doubtless counted to be his natural and mortal foes.

But my Lord,—being occupied in examining the river—observed nothing, and having presently found another place where the water was shallow, he desired the men to ride over carefully one by one ; which was done, himself crossing last, and all advancing up the slope, I following gladly, and rejoicing greatly within myself to have escaped from that place without worse befalling.

Nevertheless, at the top of the slope which led from the ford to the level country, my Lord paused to breathe his horse, and I, being beside him, was forced to pause likewise. The place where we had crossed the stream lay immediately below us, and the ford we had first come to, and at which that Foul Thing had been sitting, was a little way above, part hidden from sight by some small bushes, as well as by the murkiness of the air.

Suddenly as we stood there my Lord started, and looked directly towards it, screening his eyes with his hand as if to see better.

'Did'st see that, Hal?' he asked, turning to me and speaking quickly.

'See what, my Lord?' I answered, striving to answer carelessly, yet trembling in every limb so that I could scarce utter.

''Tis strange, but methought at that moment I saw a woman sitting by the brink of yonder ford; a very old woman she seemed to be, and bent almost to doubleness. Did'st see her too I ask, or did my eyes deceive me?'

'Nay my Lord' I replied tremblingly, 'I saw no such thing; moreover how could a woman of that age be out at this hour, and in so lonesome a place?'—For I feared to own that I had seen her, knowing that she had come there for no good!

'True,' replied he thoughtfully. 'And yet I surely thought I saw such an one, and moreover it seemed that she beckoned to me with her hand, like one that had somewhat to say, and that in the other hand she held something half hidden under a cloth which she lifted towards me. Strange that a man's eyes should play him such tricks, and but that the night is so dark I would ride back to the place, and see whether there be any one there or not.'

'Now for the love of God, my Lord,' I cried in terror, 'do not do so! Who knows but what some ambuscade is intended, and that these treacherous savages have set her there to lure your Lordship into their power!'

'Pish Hal!' cried he, 'either thy fears for me, or perchance thy hatred of this people misleads thee, so that thou smell'st danger in every bush, and an ambush in every ragged crone sitting harmlessly by the roadside. For a certainty, save that I expect to find yon messengers from the Queen arrived upon my return, I would ride back, and see whether it be as I thought, or whether some mere bush or brake deceived me.'

With these words his Lordship turned his horse, as it seemed reluctantly, and rode after the escort, which waited for him a few perches away.

But I—driven by what madness I know not— could not refrain from once again turning my eyes to the place, though much I loathed to do so, and sore I shook in every limb with fear of what I might behold.   And lo! that Accursed Crone was still there, only erect now, and standing upon the further brink of the river.   And it seemed to me that her stature had grown to be greater than is the stature of any mere mortal woman, so that despite the murkiness of the air I could plainly discern her lineaments, and could see the foul and livid colour of her cheeks, and mark her thin and wrinkled chaps, which seemed to be moving up and down with a deadly and a mocking smile as she looked after us.   And in one hand she held something covered with a cloth, the shape of which, so far as I could discern it, appeared to be that of a human head, newly severed from the trunk, and dripping at the neck with blood, which as she held it aloft, fell down drop by drop into the river running below.   Nor was this [though enough] all, nor the worst, no nor the half even of what I saw, for as God is my witness, and as I hope, being a

sinful man, to be saved by His Grace at the last
day, so I do here solemnly protest and declare
that this gory head which she held thus aloft in
her hands appeared to me as I gazed at it to be
the very image and presentment of my dear Lord
the Earl's own head, only that the cheeks were of
a ghastly hue, like those of a man new dead, and
that the eyes of it seemed to be tight shut, and all
sunk, hollow, and half hidden in the head !

Then, when that fearful vision met my sight,
all the blood in my own body seemed to forsake it,
and I reeled to and fro in the saddle like a man
drunk with wine, so that I marvel how I fell not
off the horse, for the river and its banks, and the
ground above it, and all that moved upon the
ground, became suddenly to me like mist and
vapour, rolling horribly along without form or
sensible substance.

And for the remainder of that ride, whether
my Lord spake or spake not, or by what road we
travelled, or what things we saw by the way, of all
this I know and can recall nothing ; for I was like
one that is carried upon the waves of a stormy sea,
my mind being so full of confusion and trouble,
and of great terror, and heaviness. Nay, what I
most resembled was a man heavily beset by

hideous dreams, who cries out and trembles in his sleep, yet knows not why he does so, or what those things are that so oppress him. And thus I continued all the remainder of the way, till we once more came before the castle of Garrett Fleminge, where old Brace, my Lord's chief body-servant, coming hastily out to the front door, cried to him in a loud voice that the messengers sent to her Majesty had newly arrived from Dredagh, and were waiting to deliver their charges unto him in the main hall.

XVIII

HEARING this his Excellency sprang from his
horse, and went quickly up the stairs to this hall,
which was upon the second floor of the castle ;
while I turned away, under pretence that I had to
see to the bestowing of the horses, but in reality
to compose my disordered visage, which would else
of a certainty, I knew, have betrayed me.

Hardly however had I dismounted, before old
Brace came running down again with a scared face,
and besought me to return to his Lordship, saying
that the messengers from her Majesty, who had
been awaiting his return in the hall, had upon
his entrance delivered over their packets into his
hands. But scarce had he broken the seals and
begun to master their contents than he was seized,
said Brace, with violent choler, and fell into such
paroxysms of anger that the very form of his
countenance was changed, and none of those
around durst approach him.—

'And, 'cept you find a way to quiet him Master Harvey,' quoth he, 'we greatly fear that a may do himself a mischief; for a rageth to and fro the room most like some bull fresh 'scaped its keepers, and for these new men about him, they be such a set of faint-hearted losels that at sight of his transports they are like to swoon away themselves for very terror!'

Then I answered him that I would come speedily; so, mounting the stairs I came into the main hall.

But when I had reached the door I too stood still, not daring to advance a step further. For my Lord was standing in the middle of the floor, holding in his hands those letters newly received from her Majesty. And his countenance in that short space of time had indeed so changed that a stranger had scarce known it for the same. And ever and anon he stamped upon the floor with his foot, and a great cry escaped his lips, as if his soul was afire, and must needs find vent, lest it burst. And—'Villains! Villains!' cried he; and again, 'Would God, I had you here!' And again —'Oh God, that I should be so mocked!' And presently,—starting from where he stood,—he strode to and fro the room like one that is tor-

mented and driven of evil spirits. And once a
settle, placed near the fire, came across him, which
he, plucking suddenly aside, broke between his
hands, as a child might break an oaten toy, yet
knew not, it seemed, that he had done so.

While he thus raged, and while I, all trembling
and amazed, stood watching him, the storm [which
had been gathering ever since we crossed that ford
of the Lagan,] rose and grew till the fury of it
appeared to fill the entire earth. For the whole
floor of Heaven was by this time darkened, so
that there was no light left, save only the light
of the fire, and some faint ruddiness which still
burned in the West. And ever and again a great
rush of wind would come hurtling over the castle,
so that it seemed like to drive in the very walls
thereof.

And I, standing there, knew not which to fear
most, the fury of the elements without, or this
sudden anger of my Lord within. For his
wrath—(though of late years less easily excited
than it was wont to be) still upon occasion, and
when he is moved beyond his common, towers to
an height such as I have never seen in any other
man, and which is more like the rage of angry
elements than that of any merely mortal creature.

And so we remained for the space of some ten minutes, I not daring to approach him, lest I should thereby but increase his wrath, or perchance draw it down upon myself.

At last—spying me—he came over; and, catching me by the wrist, pulled me forward into the room, looking into my face the while without speaking; his eyes opening and flashing, as you may see the eyes of an hawk open and flash when it is about to strike.

So—trembling with apprehension—'What is it my Lord?' I asked. 'What in God's name moves your Lordship to this sudden heat of choler?'

'Rascality, Hal!' he answered, 'Villainy! False Swearing! Calumny! those are what have moved me! Oh 'tis naught,' cried he, suddenly loosing hold of me, and beginning to pace the chamber to and fro as he had done before.— ''Tis naught that the Queen should heap railing accusations upon me, as if it rested with me alone to lay hands upon Tyrone, and bring him in chains before her. 'Tis naught that she should assail me with heart-wounding words, as if every mishap that hath befallen this curst land during the last twenty years lay wholly at my charge. But 'Sdeath! that

she should do this! Hell and furies, that she
should forbid my return! That she should with-
draw the license freely of herself given, and forbid
my availing myself of it. Forbid it! Nay 'tis not
she! 'tis those lying, intriguing knaves that have
stolen into her ear, and would use her now for their
own purposes. Look Hal! look at this! and see
if betwixt every line of her Majesty's you read not
at least ten lines of these plotters, that would fain
twist and turn her to their own ends?'

With that his Lordship thrust the letter he
had been reading into my hands, pointing as he
did so to certain lines, which he commanded me to
read aloud, and which ran as follows—

'—Because by your return many and great
confusions may follow, our Will and Pleasure is,
and we do upon your Duty command you, that,
notwithstanding our former License provisionally
given——'

'Provisionally! 'twas not provisionally!' cried
he, 'as I am a gentleman and a man of honour
'twas absolutely and freely offered by herself, and
given to me in writing when I went to take my
leave! But read on, I say; read on!'—

'—Whereby you have liberty to return, and
to constitute some temporary governor in your

absence, we forbid you now to take that liberty, or to adventure to leave the State in any person's government, save with our Allowance first had of him, and our Pleasure known to you, without which Allowance you are by no means to come out of that Kingdom, by virtue of any former license whatsoever.'

'There! There! see you their excellent device?' he cried snatching up the paper, 'they think—Raleigh, Cobham, and the rest—that they have me mewed safely up for ever and ever in this beggarly island! That Essex will stand patient as a hooded falcon, which allows the quarry to be filched from under its very beak! That mischance has so trod his fortunes down that he must bend the knee to those that but use the Queen's name for their own devices. But they Doat, Hal! they Doat! Essex is no child to be mocked; no moulting haggard or sorry forked kite to be driven from his quarry! Essex will descend upon them when they least expect it! Aye, will he; fast as ship's sails, and swift horses can take him.'

'Nay, my Lord,' I cried, my fears in his behalf moving me to forget my own late terror. 'Nay my Lord, you will never return to England, having

S

under your hand her Majesty's plain and express command to remain where you are. To do so, believe me, would be to run into peril; seeing that her Majesty, as all know, brooks not disobedience.'

'Peril!' shouted he at the top of his voice, 'Peril quotha! Now by the sword of my father I thought you knew me better, Hal! Peril! Since ever you knew Essex—which methinks was not yesterday—did'st ever know him to be hindered by any such cowards' bugs and trumpery as that? Why man, for a nothing—for mere sport, and to quiet the too free leaping and pricking of the blood—how often have I fronted, and you know it a hundred such perils, aye and dared fifty foes any of them of greater weight than these that would affront me! Pooh man, talk not to me of peril! The very word, the thought, is like meat and drink to me! It warms my blood like wine to think how I will surprise them; aye, as a lion surprises some petty hunter, who believes him to be afar off, and suddenly hears him roaring at his elbow.'

'But her Majesty, my Lord?' quoth I, all tremblingly.

'Her Majesty? Oh beshrew me, Hal, her

Majesty will be glad enough to see me, of that I am assured. Nay I would wager my Earl's baldrick to the straw girdle of one of yonder kernes that I shall have half these plotters ducking at my knee ere I be three hours in the Court!'

'I hope to Heaven it may be so, my Lord,' said I doubtfully.

'You hope! Marry, Hal, but I *know* it to be so. And were it not—were my head to pay the forfeit —yet would I go. I tell thee my soul is on fire till I can reach them. What? Would they screen themselves behind the Queen's petticoats? shoot out their arrows at me from behind that rampart? steal into her ear, rob me of my reward, and in the end laugh at my beard? Nay, but I will stop their springes ere they grow too proud! My hand shall be upon them, and that right swiftly.'

'Alas my Lord' I said, 'what I fear is that those who hate you have planned this device for that very purpose, knowing your fiery nature, and hoping that, you presenting yourself without license before her Majesty, may seem but to approve their calumnies.'

'Not so, Hal, you mistake the matter utterly. For, look you, their guile is like the guile of boys setting springes for birds, or like that of some base

s 2

churl, who would fain enmesh some free forest
beast, which, save by treachery, he durst not
approach. Face them, Hal ; face them, and their
power is over ! And for this prohibition that so
frights you, believe me they have but enchanted
it into her Majesty's mind, hoping that by means
of it I shall be forced to remain here, obeying
what seems her order, but in reality is theirs ; they
lurking behind her image, as small and indifferent
actors on the Greek stage were wont to hide their
pettiness under some large and stately mask.
Oh, sweet knaves, I know you ! Your craft ; your
cunning ; your plotting device ! Keep Essex in
Ireland ! Keep him in prison ! Keep him in Hell !
Oh clever devices ! Oh crafty Councillors ! I
know you ! I know you !'

Then was I silent, fearing only to increase his
anger, and not knowing, in truth, what to say, or
how to say it. But he, walking to and fro the
room, broke ever and anon into a laugh, as if some
new thought was stirring within him, the image of
which was less displeasing than cheerful, and even
mirth-producing.

And presently—' Fore God, what children and
blown dandelion tufts we are !' cried he. ' Know
you, good fellow, that that one little word of yours,

" Peril," hath done me more good than would a brace of leeches at my elbow, each with a purge in the one hand and a lancet in the other! For my brain, which a while back was so clogged that it seemed charged with molten lead, now again moves freely, and I feel the blood mount and spin lightly, as the sap does through the trees in spring. Nay my wits seem clearer than their wont, so that I can see what shall befal ere it come to pass, and enjoy my triumph while as yet it is far off. I laugh, Hal, I laugh to think of their faces when they shall behold me! While the dull fools are plotting my overthrow, and hatching schemes how to poison her Majesty's mind against me—all for her good and the Kingdom's weal!—suddenly in I walk! hot from travel; fresh from my Irish adventures; hat on head; sword on side; boots bespattered to the knees; with a—" Gentlemen, good day! Your humble servant!" Ha ha ha! See you their faces Hal? See you them ? Ha ha ha! Ha ha ha!'

Then I was the more afraid, for his laughter seemed to me of scarce less dangerous omen than his rage awhile back. And in my heart I prayed for strength to be able to utter words which migh dissuade my dear Lord—if any words of mine could by possibility do so—from that course upon which he was then entering. But, just as I was about to speak, he, growing suddenly grave, turned upon me ere I could utter two words.

'Hold thy tongue Hal ; hold thy tongue !' cried he, 'For I can see the remonstrances growing upon thy lips, but I tell thee my mind is made up to go, and though King Solomon himself stood there in thy image he would not avail to dissuade me. Nay, the more thou fearest my impetuosity the more should'st thou desire my departure, for the longer I delay the hotter grows my wrath, and the deeper and the deadlier will be my revenge. Oh, you placid ones understand us little, believe me ! Know that there are depths in natures like mine, that it scares even myself to peer into, and to lean over ! An I be so wronged that I can by no means right myself, nor yet see justice upon those that injure me, I have it in me to take a vengeance —such a vengeance that our babes' grandchildren will be talking of it still ! Aye have I, a vengeance such as no subject hath taken yet ; one that will cause London itself to run red in blood up to the very doorsteps !'

'Now for the love of Heaven, my Lord' I cried in terror, 'For the love of God and all good angels go not yet awhile! Wait till the first rush of your wrath is abated! Wait a little, only a little. Wait till you hear again from her Majesty, and some fresh matter arise. Wait I implore you! of such haste no good ever cometh.'

'Wait, Hal? What parrot cry is this? Wait? Not I! not a day, nor an hour. Were it not that the night is already advanced I would depart this very moment, and of a certainty not later than tomorrow morning by first crow of cock. And, the time being short, and there being few he.e with me, I purpose to take but a couple of gentlemen ushers, and some ten at most of the serving men. But you will I leave behind me in Ireland for the present.'

'Leave me behind you, my Lord!' cried I. 'Nay, since you must needs go, take me at least along with you. Sure what sin have I committed that my Lord should thus suddenly deny me his service?'

'Sin, Hal? no sin,' he replied impatiently. 'Nor do I misdoubt your love; nay for that reason leave I you behind me, so that I may for a certainty hear what befalls after my absence, and have one here on whom I may rely, and with whom I can hold communication. But we waste time! Fetch hither your writing tables, and write quickly to my dictation, for I must forthwith despatch messengers to Dredagh, to warn them that be there of my coming tomorrow, that they prepare betimes to meet me.'

Then was I forced to obey, seeing that he would list to naught, or so much as give ear even to any counsel that I durst offer. Yet did I do so with a reluctant heart, and a sore and deeply perturbed mind ; seeming to see his overthrow chained, as it were by Destiny, to this his sudden, and most unhappy resolve.

For the more I reflected upon the whole matter the more it grew clear to my mind that in this opposition to her Majesty there lurked for him some great and deadly peril. 'For' said I to myself, 'such direct disobedience to the very letter of her commands is more than any Sovereign upon earth could stomach, especially one that has never encountered so much as the very breath of opposition without straightway chastising it rudely.' And the thought of all that might yet arise out of this matter grew upon me till my breath began to come in quick pants, and my hands to grow cold, and a great creeping come over me, beginning at the outside of my

skin, and reaching in even to the innermost parts
of my body.

But all that night, until the very whiteness of
dawn was shining afresh in the sky, my Lord
continued to walk to and fro that hall; now and
again pausing to dictate some portion of a letter
to me; yet, ere one letter was fairly finished,
beginning at another; then breaking off to call to
him one of the serving men or gentlemen ushers,
or to give some fresh charges concerning this
journey which was to begin upon the morrow.

For my part, though I strove to follow his
instructions, yet my mind so wandered that at
times I could scarce understand what he said.
For whether it was the remembrance of what I
had seen that afternoon, or the want of natural
sleep, or the beginning of that sickness of which I
afterward suffered many things, or the mere cold
of that gloomy hall, or whatever the cause was,
certain it is that long ere dawn I was like a man
that shakes and shivers in the grip of some deadly
fever, so that I could scarce see the very letters
that lay under my eyes, and that my own hand
had written. Nay, so perturbed was I, that even
natural things came to seem unnatural to me, so
that often I felt as if the room were suddenly

filled with antic creatures, mopping and mowing, and moving hurriedly to and fro with crazy leaps.

And, this perturbation increasing ever more and more, at last everything ; even the wind which roared over the roof, and the trees which swayed and bent without ; nay the mere crackling of the torches, and movements within doors, caused me to start and shiver like a frightened coney, and my sweat to stand out in big drops, as you may see the drops of dew stand upon the twigs of a morning. And getting worse and worse as the night advanced, it came at length to this that I durst hardly so much as lift up my eyes from the table at which I sat, lest I should suddenly behold some Red-headed Demon of this country peering in at us with fiery eyes, or, worse still, some foul Witch Creature smiling with yellow and withered lips, the smile of one who smiles and beckons on another unto his Doom !

XIX

ALL that night, while my Lord and I sat writing, there was great running to and fro in the castle, for his Excellency had given orders that everything should be in readiness by the first dawn of day. And, having lain down about three o'clock for the space of some two hours, by six in the morning he was in the saddle, and by eleven of the same forenoon we rode into the town of Dredagh.

Here he quickly summoned a Council, and gave over the chief charge of all things in the North to Sir Samuel Bagenal, commanding also Sir Warham St. Leger and others who were there to aid and support him, each in their several degrees. He likewise despatched Sir William Warren to the Earl of Tyrone with news of his departure, but all had to be done in great haste, so that there was scant time for any man to know what he had to do, so firmly was my Lord set upon riding forward that same day, no man daring to say him nay, his resolution being so plainly written out upon his face.

Nevertheless, there being much to see to and many hindrances, it came to be five in the afternoon ere we again set forth from Dredagh to ride to Dublin ; I having with some difficulty obtained his Excellency's license to accompany him as far as the ship.

The first part of our road being very bad we were forced to go slowly, so that darkness came down upon us ere we had ridden far ; the weather too continued very wet, and the wind exceeding high, only that being at our backs it aided us forward rather than impeded us. And at the first halting place his Excellency would not delay a moment, but having procured fresh horses galloped on ; and the same thing happened at the second also ; for, though earnestly pressed to tarry, and to recruit his strength with some food and wine, he refused, and pressed on, seeming to be driven as it were by some constraining power, which forbad him either to eat or to rest until his journey was accomplished.

So—like unto some company flying for their lives, who ride and ride and durst not look behind them—rode we ; the rain slanting against our faces, the wind howling at our backs, the horses stumbling, and now and then one falling, through slipping in some deep rut, or being bogged in the foul and marshy ground. And about nine of the clock, the moon flashing suddenly out, Lo! the sea lay below us, looking all cold, white, and naked in its rays, and about an hour, or perchance an hour and a half later we halted at last before the walls of Dublin.

But when, all wearied out and worn with hard riding, we drew rein before the North gate, at first the sentries refused positively to admit us, not knowing who we were, or from whence we had come. And when, after long delay and difficulty we had at last got in, and it was noised abroad that his Excellency had arrived, [he being expected of no man,] then suddenly, and despite the lateness of the hour, a great buzz and commotion spread about the town. And some cried out that Tyrone had been defeated ; while others said nay, that it was his Excellency who had been defeated, and that only he himself and we that were with him had escaped alive out of the slaughter ; while others said they knew not what, only that some Great Matter had occurred. And the whole city

was like an anthill newly overturned, no two agreeing as to what had happened ; but all, getting up
out of their beds, ran hither and thither, and dis-
puted one with another, no man knowing further
than his own worthless opinion ; until the rain,
growing suddenly worse, drave them back to their
beds again.

By this time the wind, which had blown hard
all day, had altogether fallen, and there was a great
stillness.   So still was it that, having persuaded
my Lord to take some rest, I—standing beside the
window of the Castle of Dublin—could hear no
sound, only the dripping of the rain which fell
from the roof, and the sudden cries of the sentries
upon the bridge, and now and then a hollow
moaning noise, which came from I know not where,
nor could discover.

Moreover I very soon found that, despite the
weariness engendered by that long ride, I should
win no sleep that night.   For whether it was from
the weight of the air and from my own disordered
spirits, I was so oppressed that I lay tossing to and
fro, being filled with feverish imaginations, which
nipped at me as it were with claws, until at last
I could have sworn that noisome creatures were
crawling up out of that black moat which lay

around the castle, and coming nearer and nearer to where I lay. And when I rose up very early the next morning lo! the stones of which its walls are built were streaked and stained with livid spots, as if a black sweat had broken out upon them. And all those trunkless heads set upon stakes over the arches and before the windows, being heavy with the night's rain, dripped continually, so that by moments they seemed to start and move, as the great drops fell from off their thick and thatch-like glibbes. And, being already so sick and distraught, I seemed to myself as I gazed at them to be as it were a ghost among ghosts, or a dead man amongst dead men, so that scarce I knew what was real, and what but the mere phantom of my own disordered spirit.

Then in the morning, before I had time to go to his Excellency, old Brace [who of all of lower station is the one whom he trusts most, and who is most worthy to be trusted] came to me, and having made sure none could overhear him, opened his mind to me familiarly, as his way is—

''Od's light! but there is some right prime villainy afoot here, Master Harvey,' said he, ' though what it bodes I know not, only that 'tis for sure directed against my Lord.'

'What mean you?' said I surprised, 'and what particular villainy do you suspect?'

'To know that,' replied he, 'would need a sharper-set nose than mine. I can smell a rat as fast as any man, but it needs a better trained terrier to know what rat's tricks it is after. Only this I tell ye, Master Harvey, which belike may be news t' you. Know you that there is a second way into this same Dublin Castle by means of a small sallyport hard by yon Birmingham tower?'

'No' said I, 'I knew it not, but if there be, what then?'

'Marry this' he answered. 'Last night about an hour after we got in, word was brought to me that Suleiman, my Lord's chief horse, was sore strained and galled; as well a might be, the poor brute, coming off such a hag-ridden road, and going at such a godless pace, albeit riderless. So —knowing my Lord would liefer lose ten pounds in gold than that ought hindered Suleiman going with him to England—I bade the lad back, and said I would follow him to the stabling place and see what must be done. But when I got out— curse me, but the rain, Master Harvey, was like a wet mop in a man's face, and having no light I was sore set to find the way. And as I was

staggering along; presently I heard a step behind
me, and looking round saw one steal softly 'gainst
the wall, having a lantern in 's hand, half hid
under 's cloak. "What's to do here in the Fiend's
name?" thought I. So I hid behind a sort of
buttress-place, and waited till he should pass.
And a crept along, Master Harvey, not going
straight like a man, but on all fours like a thief,
and now and then a wriggled a bit on 's belly, like
a sick cat, till a came to a little door half hid in th'
outer castle wall. And when a got to it a worked
a while till a got it open. And then I looked hard,
and saw six men coming up one after t'other, as
'twere out of th' entrails of th' earth. And most
of them were strangers to me, or in the dark
seemed so, but just at the last the lantern gave a
sort of a twist, and the light struck the hinder-
most, and that he was one Lance Renshaw, who
is serving man to Sir Henry Oldcastle, and that
we left him behind us yesternight at Dredagh
that I dare swear.'

' This is a strange tale, Brace ' said I. ' And it
seems scarce likely that such as you describe would
have followed so close upon our heels, we having
ridden so hard and the ways being so foul.'

' Like or not like, Master Harvey ' he answered,

T

'I tell ye 'twas he. For, look ye, I was standing yester forenoon in the main street of Dredagh with Nat Gregory, and cursing a bit belike at the suddenness of our setting forth, my bones being so crusty ever since I was nigh lost in that river by Waterford. And just then I spied this flap-eared fellow Lance Renshaw peeping at us round the corner. May I be hanged for a half-penny if I didn't ! Why bless your heart, Master Harvey I should know the rogue's face of him if he hid it under a bishop's mitre, or dressed it up in a woman's coif, marry would I.'

' May be,' said I, ' still I doubt but you mistook him either here or there. Why, man, 'tis as much as anyone's life is worth to follow my Lord secretly as you describe. Were he to get wind of it 'tis not the greatness of his estate, let him be who he would, that would keep him five minutes from his vengeance.'

' Tut, tut, Master Harvey ! ' said he impatiently. ' I tell ye there's a many things go on here and elsewhere of which my Lord knows little enough. And since y'are so hard to persuade, just you come with me an' I'll show you a peep hole where you may look into a place in this very castle we be standing in where, an I be not far wrong, they do at this moment hatch some fresh villainy against him ; though what that villainy be I know not, not being, I thank God, a politician, nor kin to any of the breed.'

With that he led the way, and I followed along a narrow passage, and up one or two flights of stairs, till we came to what had once seemingly been the outer wall of the castle, for it was pricked here and there with small holes, doubtless for the discharging of bolts or arrows. Most of these holes had been filled up with stones, but so roughly that they stood out clear from the surface ; and in one place half of them had been picked out again, seemingly in mischief or idleness, so that by pushing his head through a man could look down and see what lay below.

Brace having signed to me to do this, I thrust in my head. But at first saw nothing, the wall being so thick, the hole itself small, and the depth below us very great. Presently—thrusting my head yet further forward, and craning my neck nigh to cracking—I was able to discern a small room some thirty or perhaps forty feet below where we stood, and that in this room were certain gathered together, though who they were I could not tell, the hole being so high above them that only the tops of their hats were discernible, which hats they wore pulled low down over their faces.

So I waited, thinking that something might hap to reveal them to me. And so it chanced, for presently one, who at first had been seated, rose to his feet, and, fronting the others, spoke to them earnestly for several minutes. To whom the rest listened eagerly, yet not, it seemed to me, as if wholly agreeing with him. Whereupon—being anxious perhaps to convince them—in the earnestness of his discourse he pushed his hat suddenly back from his brows, so that I could see the face of him, which stood out under the shadow of it, thin, sallow, and sharp-nosed as a ferret's. And then, sure enough, I knew him! as would any other man in Ireland, he being at this time the most talked of upon the Queen's side, bating my Lord, in that whole kingdom ; whose name out of respect for his office I give not, only this much will I say, that he is known to all men as a sure and a constant unfriend to his Excellency.

Finding presently that I could hear nothing, because of the great depth which separated me from those below, I drew back, sore disquieted, and considering deeply what 'twere best to do in the matter. 'For,' thought I, 'if I go to my Lord,

and make him 'ware of who is here, and what
manner of secret council they hold within the
very walls of the castle, his wrath assuredly will
spring abroad like a ball of wild fire, and who
knows but what it may cause him to do or say
something that may yet further imperil his cause
before her Majesty ? '

Having charged old Brace therefore to repeat
to no man what had been seen and heard, I passed
on to his Excellency's bed-chamber. But the
minute I entered he began giving me orders, so
that all might be in readiness for the morning,
when and not an hour later, he said, he was resolved
to sail. Whereupon [first humbly intreating his
pardon for my forwardness] I prayed him once
more very earnestly to consider his resolve, and to
delay his going, were it but for a few days and till
fresh advices came from her Majesty ; saying that
I knew for a certainty that some ill thing was in
the wind ; and that those who loved him least were
the ones most anxious that he should immediately
depart.

At this he at first mocked ; asking how long
I had been a soothsayer, and so deep in the con-
fidence of statesmen, and that it was plain I knew
more of such matters than he did himself. To

which I replied that I made no pretensions either
to statecraft nor yet to soothsaying, but that my
love for him was like the drawing of the magnet
to the pole, and enabled me, [being myself small
and of little importance,] to point out the path to
one greater than myself, who might otherwise have
missed it.   Finding that, though he smiled, my
words had no weight with him, if indeed he
listened to them, I presently expounded to him
fully all that I had seen and suspected, and all
that old Brace had seen the night before.   At the
hearing of which he grew, not angry, but rather
meditative, as if some thought which was not
altogether new to him were stirring again, and
moved him to thoughtfulness.

All at once, smiting his two hands together
—'Too late! too late,' cried he.   'A truce to
reflection !   On, either in God's name, or the
Devil's.   On, though the winds be never so high ;
though the sails crack, and the waves roar !   That
I am encompassed with traitors and treachery I
need neither you, nor Brace, nor any other soothsayer to tell me.   Marry, what then ?   The more
numerous and subtle my foes the greater the need
of boldness on my part, so that I may overmatch
them.   I tell thee, Hall, I am sick, sick to death of

these eternal rocks! I will e'en now crowd all sail, and so reach some secure haven, or, if it must be, founder quickly. By mine oath I care not so very greatly which it be!'

'Those who love you care then, my Lord!' cried I, passionately.

'Do they Hal? Some few perchance; you, for example, kind heart; for you your Essex's ship, I do believe, is even as your own, and carries all your merchandise.'

'Aye, my Lord' said I, 'and hath this many a long year past.'

'True Hal, and for that reason I grieve if mischance befal for your sake, and for the sake of some few more that love me. For myself, I tell you honestly I care little. Nay, there have been moods of late in which I have felt like some luckless diver of the Orient, who, having lost his all, resolves to make one last plunge, and either bring back with him some pearl of great price, or else never again be seen upon the surface.'

When I heard these words and saw the look with which he uttered them, my heart seemed suddenly to sink within me, thinking of that fair head of his, which so long had been the daystar of my life, being lost and quenched in the envious waves. And at the thought and the image it aroused a great sob broke suddenly from my bosom ; at sound of which my Lord looked up, seemingly not a little astonished, and then smiled, saying—

'There, there! trouble not thyself poor soul! I did but speak in jest. Nay, comfort thee! comfort thee, I say! Sure am I that every pulse in thy body beats true to thine Essex. Is 't not so ? '

'God knows it, my Lord! God knows it!' cried I. 'He knows that though I be no fighter, nor boast myself braver than other men, yet would I gladly shed every drop of blood in my veins, here, now, immediately at your feet, rather than that my dear Lord should run into this deadly peril upon which his soul seems to be so bent.'

'Gramercy, my poor fellow, thy blood would be of little avail methinks !' replied he still smilingly. And then he seemed to muse awhile, as if in doubt, not knowing what to decide upon. Whereupon, [fancying that even now and at the last he might be about to yield to my entreaties], I suddenly dropped before him upon my two knees, stretching out my hands to him and crying—
'Master! dear Master! Essex! sweet Lord! Be wrath with thy servant, but hearken to him this once, only this once! Quit this mad resolve!

Go not I pray you; for the love of God go not! For of a surety I see your overthrow chained as if by rivets to this your going!'

At that his countenance changed, and—'Enough sir! This is mere midsummer madness!' cried he angrily. 'Go to, Mr. Harvey you displease me! Not a word more! What I have said that I have said, and what I have resolved, that do I intend to fulfil. Go to; carry out those orders that I have given you, and see that all is in readiness against the morning; for by my oath there has been but too much delay already.'

Then, [seeing plainly that I could effect nothing, but only angered him,] I rose up from my knees very ruefully, and moved toward the door, feeling as if a mountain were piled above my head, and my heart and my limbs were broken down under the weight of the same. But—just as I was leaving the door, and ere it closed behind me—I fancied that he spoke again, so waited; thinking that he might have some further commands to give me.

Finding that he did not speak—'You called me, my Lord?' said I hesitatingly.

'Aye Hal, did I. I . . . I would . . .'

Breaking suddenly off in what he was about to say, he rose from his seat, and, crossing the

room, came rapidly over to me, holding out his
hand. 'Hal!' cried he, 'Honest Hal! wish me
God speed!' And the last word he uttered
hurriedly, like one that is seized with some sudden
alarm or misgiving, which he himself understands
not, yet can by no means wholly resist. And
taking hold of my hand, he wrung it suddenly
to and fro. Whereupon for very fulness of heart
I could not speak, for my eyes so overflowed, that
for several minutes I saw neither him nor ought
else that was in the room.

Which—he perceiving—'See how one coward
makes two!' cried he smiling. 'Behold how the
shadow of your fears, my faithful Hal, has for one
instant all but overpeered the well-piled mountain
of my own resolution! Yet am I resolved to
go! hap what may ; come what will ; resolved to
go, and to out-face them all! For look you, I
have a heat in me, a kind of natural fire, so that
the very thought of those things of which they
falsely accuse me—Liars, cowards, villains that they
are !—God's life ! when that thought rises before
me, it so fills my brain that I seem to burn inwardly, and would fain not think of it, lest the
revenge I plan recoil first upon myself, and drive
me mad!'

'Think not of it then at all, and for God's sake be calm, my Lord,' cried I. For in truth I could see by his eyes and the sudden flushing of his face that his thoughts were too tightly strung for his own good ; and much I feared that, arriving in such wrath, and coming when none looked for him, he would but play the advocate to his enemies, and seem to give their calumnies substance.

'True, Hal! I will be calm !—calm as water ere it bursts its ice ! calm as Etna when the lava within is at the hottest !—Oh they shall find me calm enough I warrant you ! But go now, go, and get all ready for tomorrow. And list, Hal, since you will not bid me God-speed, I at least on my side will bid God bless you, for a truer friend and servant never hot, impatient master found. And if mischance befal me, you may at least comfort yourself by thinking that 'twas no doing of yours, and that I went not without abundant warning to hinder me.'

'Oh my Lord! my Lord!' cried I, 'Sorry comfort were that to me if ought befel you, which may God in His infinite pity and mercy avert, and so bring my foolish previsions to nothingness, as I heartily hope and pray.'

'Why there! that is well spoken!' cried he.

' Beshrew me, lad, but we shall have many a loud laugh over this yet! Methinks when thou and I are a pair of solemn old grey-beards, these terrors of thine will serve to adorn some tale told to our grandsons over the yule fire, while the flap-dragons splutter, and the maids ply distaffs, and all goes merry in the Hall. But haste away now! haste thee, I say; or our matters are like to be behindhand in the morning. Suddenly, sweet Hal! Suddenly!'

*   *   *   *   *   *

XX

THEN next morning being come, by six of the clock all who were of my Lord's company and following were astir to accompany him to the ship, the Captain of the Queen's sloop, whom he had desired privately to be in readiness, having sent word that the tide would only serve up to the hour of eleven at latest.

By this time, it must be understood, many other knights and gentlemen, besides those who had ridden with us from Dredagh, had gathered about his Excellency; the greater part of those that had accompanied him from England being desirous to return thither in his company; of whom the most notable were my Lords of Southampton, and Rutland; also the Lord Dunkellin who is son to the Earl of Clanricarde, with sundry others, all full of great zeal and love for his service.

But when we arose in the morning, lo! a great mist or sea fog covered all the neighbourhood of the Castle of Dublin, so that the town below it seemed to have wholly melted and vanished away in the night time.   And when he left his chamber my Lord could see nothing, neither could we that were with him ; so that we staggered in our going, falling one against another, and torches had to be lit that we might find our way.   So strange and unnatural-looking a morning I have never seen ; and a great weight was thereby laid upon the spirits of all ; which [if I dare judge others by myself], were none too light and cheerfully-disposed already.

Hearing that certain of the Council, as well as the Lord Mayor and aldermen of the city, with the pensioners, and other gentlemen, were assembled to greet his Excellency and to kiss his hands (they not yet knowing that he was about to leave them) he presently passed into the great hall ; which hall is mostly used for the assembling of Council, and the delivering of proclamations ; we that were with him following, each one in his order.

But when we had got into the hall no man could see who was there, or who was not ; for the fog had filled it to the very walls, it being large, and sparingly pierced with windows.   Accordingly we stood staring round, being able to see that a considerable company was certainly gathered there, but not able to discern so much as one of their faces. Moreover it seemed as if some weight or impediment lay upon them ; no man stepping blithely forward to greet my Lord, but all hanging back together in a great cluster, as if each was wishful that some other should be the first to tender his duty and obedience.

Observing this, his Excellency stood still a minute, as if surprised. Presently, clapping his hands together, he called with a loud voice for more torches to be brought. And when the men that carried them came running in, he ordered that they should stand at intervals round about the hall, so as to lighten it ; and that others, to the number of six or eight, should gather about himself, and throw their lights forward, so that he might be able for a certainty to discern whom he was addressing.

This being done he advanced up the middle of the hall, the Earl of Southampton and other gentlemen that were to sail with him keeping close beside him, their swords, spurs, and other accoutrements making a great jingling noise as they moved across the pavement. My Lord himself wore on this occasion his suit of black armour, and over it a loose velvet surcoat embroidered in pearls, which surcoat had been made for him two years since in Prague ; the sleeves of it very wide, hanging in the oriental fashion nearly to his knees ; the buttons each a great pearl, set about with smaller ones in the semblance of a rose or chamomile flower.

When he had got into the centre of the hall, and saw that all eyes were earnestly intent upon him, he stood still again, and held up his hand, to indicate that he had somewhat of importance to say. And, this done, he brake to them his coming departure, of which up to then none had known anything, save by rumours ; telling them that it was expedient that he should go, seeing that the service of her Majesty and of the State required it ; but not entering into the causes that led to this his sudden resolution, and speaking in such peremptory-wise that none who heard him durst reply, however they might inwardly be astonished at the same.

Then—leaving them all open-mouthed and staring—he passed on into an inner chamber ; and, having summoned before him the Council, he made over the government of Ireland to the Lord

Chancellor and the Treasurer; also to Dr. Adam
Loftus, the Archbishop, appointing all three of
them to be Lords Justices. For the command of
the army, this he resigned into the hands of the
Earl of Ormonde; who, not being in Dublin at the
time, had to be written to in all haste to Kilkenny;
nor knew anything of what had befallen till my
Lord was already far upon his road to London.

By this time it was near ten of the clock,
and—the horses standing ready and saddled at
the door—all who were to accompany my Lord
to the sloop mounted, and rode out by the great
gate of the Castle; he having to take boat at the
same place, namely the *Ring's End*, at which we
had disembarked upon our arrival. For by no
ordinary tide can any ship drawing over five feet
of water advance to the quays of Dublin, but must
lie ever out at this *Ring's End*; moreover even
there the haven falleth almost wholly dry with
every ebb, so that a man may walk dry foot, 'tis
said, round the ships; saving only at two places,
one on the North, called the Pool of Clontarf, and
one upon the South called the Poolbeg; which two
places do run never dry, but ships can lie there
readily afloat in as much as nine and ten feet of water.

Having got beyond the walls of the city, sud-

U

denly the fog seemed to roll down upon us with greater volume than before; falling over and over in vast scrolls and circles of vapour. Yet, it being somewhat higher in air, we found it easier to discern our footing, which was fortunate, this way from Dublin to the *Ring's End* being a very dangerous one, the sea water at every high tide invading it, leaving only a narrow passage, most easily to be missed, especially in foul weather. As befel indeed on this occasion, though not to us. For no sooner was it noised abroad through Dublin that my Lord was for a certainty sailing that morning, than there came running out from the streets and bye-ways a great press of people, all eager to see him depart. And as many as could procure horses followed in our train, and many more that could procure no horses ran a-foot; of whom a considerable number, I was afterwards informed, missing their way in the fog, got astray amongst the pools, sands, and brackish places; and narrowly escaped drowning.

For our part, though not without some peril of the like misadventure, we attained the shore in safety; where we found that, the tide being high, the Queen's sloop had been able to be brought close up to the very edge of the quay, so that the boats had but a short way to go. My Lord having stepped himself into the first of these, accompanied by the Earl of Southampton, the rest crowded into others, as many as they could find. But me, his Excellency strictly forbad to follow him on board, fearing, I imagine, that my grief might break out too violently at the last, or perchance that I might renew my efforts to stay his going, which would only trouble him, and assuredly serve no better purpose, all being now so utterly fixed, finished and determined.

So, [being left alone upon the sea shore, with only certain of the baser sort around me, every man who could obtain licence having crowded toward the vessel,] I turned aside my head, not bearing to see the last of him whom of all men on earth I loved best, and next to God revered. And my eyes—which hitherto I had restrained, fearing to displeasure him—overflowed, so that for some minutes I could see naught, neither the sea, nor yet the ship, nor they that were about me, nor they that in boats were fast hastening after him to the sloop. But at length, hearing a stir and murmur amongst those who pressed nearest to the edge of the wharf, I too suddenly uplifted my head and looked whither the rest had gone. And lo! the ship seemed to have come much nearer to me than at first, having perchance been wafted closer by the tide. And right in front of it upon the deck stood my Lord, having lately mounted thereon, and so close seemingly that I could perceive the very whiteness of his neck where it rose above his armour. And upon either hand of him stood knights and gentlemen, as many as the sloop would hold. And behind him stood one holding aloft a great sword, which is called the Sword of State, and which he held high erect in air, and naked as the custom is. And for what reason it should have come into my mind at that moment God alone knows, who understands the secrets of our hearts, and can read those mysteries of our nature which we ourselves neither understand, nor can give any reasonable account of; but, as if in a vision, suddenly it seemed to me that this place upon which his Excellency stood was no ship at all, nor yet the deck of a ship, but a scaffold ; and that this man who bore the naked sword on high was no other than an executioner; and that he and I, and all that crowd of people, both those around him upon the ship, and those who pressed beside me upon the shore, had all come together that day to see my dear Lord die !

Now, when that thought came into my mind it was like a sharp and cruel spear piercing to the very vitals ; nay so sharp was it, and so cruel was its thrust, that with difficulty could I refrain from uttering a cry ; and only that, suddenly stretching out my hand, I caught at a stake set erect there by the fishermen for the drying of their nets, and so saved myself, assuredly I should have fallen to the ground.

But gazing now, even as a man gazeth whose last hope in this life seems to be parting from before his eyes, I saw my Lord advance and speak to the Captain ; and, having conferred with him awhile, he turned next to give his orders to those that were to remain behind in Ireland. And, as he did so, each man to whom he spoke bowed himself low before him, kissing his hand as though he had been a very prince or monarch. Yet for all this bowing and all this humility, that dreadful thought never for one moment left my mind. Nay it rather seemed to me as if they were but excusing themselves before him, as is often done when a great man comes to die, and they that are the ministers of his death do entreat his pardon, they being, as he well knows, but the ignorant instruments, and not the real, actual, and witting originators of his Doom.

The wind being at this time very favourable, although so light, the anchors that attached the ship were speedily loosed ; all who were aboard of it, but not to sail, hastening to regain the land. And no sooner was it clear of them than—like to some live thing which regains its liberty—the sloop began to move, the mists giving way before it as it advanced, and curving in behind with long loops and twisting coils of vapour, like to a brood of serpents new disturbed. And some of these coils were so high that they reached to the tops of the masts, entangling and encircling the sails so that they seemed half strangled ; and underneath them I could see the black water, bestrewn with long ropes and tassels of foam where the late storm had flung them. Then, being so bemused with my trouble, in place of watching the ship I kept staring down, I know not why, into this dark and troubled waste of water which rolled between it and me. And as I did so, suddenly it seemed to me that I saw something like a hand clutching vacantly, and then as it were an arm, which appeared rising up out of the water, and as suddenly falling back to it again. And, still gazing down like one bewildered, who knows not what he does or why he does it, little by little there grew upon me the semblance of a face, which yet was not like any human face, but so deformed and shapeless that it resembled something half created ; or rather something that had once had life, but that Death has overtaken, and has passed therefore into that foul and unsightly condition to which all, even the fairest of us, must some day come.

So, staring down perplexed and stupified—wondering in the blankness of my mind how it could be that this thing which had scarce any form at all, and at which the mind revolted utterly, should yet seem so familiar— all at once there returned to my mind the remembrance of that foul Witch or She-fiend whom I had seen in Ulster, the day that I rode out with my Lord early in the morning, and that coming back late in the afternoon we crossed the ford of the Lagan. Then, being already so weak, foolish, and devoid of comfort, when that last dreadful recollection took possession of my mind suddenly it seemed to me that I no longer cared what befel. For everything which men most strive, pant, and struggle to obtain ; everything, whether of fair repute, or of foul repute, of good or evil hap, all had in that one instant become to me as it were alike and indifferent ; Sorrow itself remaining but an idle word, something that is understood of in a dream, but fades and has become mere Nothingness by the morning. And in this mood of mine the ship and all that were upon it passed away from my sight, dissolving as a dream dissolves, or some pageant, which though it may seem to be firm for a moment, yet having once passed on, never returns again.

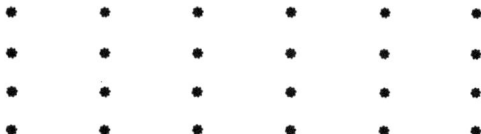

UNCOMFORTABLE; *Uncommendable! Thus suddenly, with so bald an Ending, (or rather plainly a No-Ending,) closeth the Narrative of Mr. Harvey.* Which Narrative, *far from providing its Reader with any orderly Account of what befel the Writer's Master and Patron after his return to England, leaveth the whole of this After-Portion of his History in mere Clouds, Darkness, and to the mistaken Imaginations of the Ignorant. Nevertheless, the Events which led to the Fall, End, Death, and Undoing of that Nobleman being known to all men, and the said ROBERT DEVEREUX EARL OF ESSEX a Figure familiar in some sort, it may be said, even to the eyes of the Vulgar, it seemeth needless for me at this Date to attempt to refurnish those Points wherein the above Narrative so plainly faulteth. Praying therefore the Reader to understand that, (save for the correction of certain visible and Eye-afflicting Blemishes,) no*

Portion of the foregoing Narrative must either in mistaken Kindness, or by any deeper seated Malice be ascribed to Me,

I rest that honoured Reader's Servant ; to be at all Times and in all Places by him commanded.

J. O. M.

THE END.

PRINTED BY
SPOTTISWOODE AND CO., NEW-STREET SQUARE
LONDON

The List of Titles
in the Garland Series

MARIA EDGEWORTH

1. Castle Rackrent *(1800)*

2. An Essay on Irish Bulls *(1802)*

3. Ennui *(1809)*

4. The Absentee *(1812)*

5. Ormond *(1817)*

SYDNEY OWENSON, LADY MORGAN

6. The Wild Irish Girl *(1806)*

7. O'Donnel. A National Tale *(1814)*

8. Florence Macarthy: an Irish Tale *(1818)*

9. The O'Briens and the O'Flahertys *(1817)*

10. Dramatic Sketches from Real Life *(1833)*

CHARLES ROBERT MATURIN

11. The Wild Irish Boy *(1808)*

12. The Milesian Chief *(1812)*

13. Women; or, Pour et Contre: A Tale *(1818)*

EYRE EVANS CROWE

14. To-day in Ireland *(1825)*

15. Yesterday in Ireland *(1829)*

JOHN BANIM AND MICHAEL BANIM

16. Tales, by the O'Hara Family *(1825)*

17. The Boyne Water, A Tale, by the O'Hara Family
    (1826)

18. Tales, by the O'Hara Family. Second Series *(1826)*

19. The Croppy. A Tale of 1798 *(1828)*

20. The Anglo-Irish of the Nineteenth Century *(1828)*

21. The Denounced *(1830)*

22. The Ghost-Hunter and his Family *(1833)*

23. The Mayor of Wind-Gap *and* Canvassing *(1835)*

24. The Bit O'Writin' and Other Tales *(1838)*

25. PATRICK JOSEPH MURRAY, The Life of John Banim,
    the Irish Novelist *(1857)*

GERALD GRIFFIN

26. Holland-Tide; or, Munster Popular Tales *(1827)*

27. Tales of the Munster Festivals *(1827)*

28. The Collegians *(1829)*

29. The Rivals *and* Tracy's Ambition *(1829)*

30. Tales of My Neighbourhood *(1835)*

31. Talis Qualis; or Tales of the Jury Room *(1842)*

32. DANIEL GRIFFIN, The Life of Gerald Griffin by his Brother, revised edition *(n.d.)*

WILLIAM CARLETON

33. Father Butler. The Lough Dearg Pilgrim *(1829)*

34. Traits and Stories of the Irish Peasantry *(1830)*

35. Traits and Stories of the Irish Peasantry, Second Series *(1833)*

36. Tales of Ireland *(1834)*

37. Fardorougha, the Miser; or, the Convicts of Lisnamona *(1839)*

38. The Fawn of Spring-Vale, The Clarionet, and Other Tales *(1841)*

39. Tales and Sketches Illustrating the Character of the Irish Peasantry *(1845)*

40. Valentine M'Clutchy, The Irish Agent; or, Chronicles of the Castle Cumber Property *(1847)*

41. The Black Prophet: a Tale of the Irish Famine *(1847)*

42. The Emigrants of Ahadarra: A Tale of Irish Life *(1848)*

43. The Tithe Proctor: being a Tale of the Tithe Rebellion in Ireland *(1849)*

44. The Life of William Carleton: Being His Autobiography and Letters; and an Account of his Life and Writings from the Point at which the Autobiography Breaks Off by David O'Donoghue *(1896)*

HARRIET MARTINEAU

45. Ireland *(1832)*

ANNA MARIA HALL

46. Sketches of Irish Character *(1829)*

47. Lights and Shadows of Irish Life *(1838)*

48. The Whiteboy. A Story of Ireland in 1822 *(1845)*

49. Stories of the Irish Peasantry *(1851)*

WILLIAM HAMILTON MAXWELL

50. O'Hara; or 1798 *(1825)*

51. The Fortunes of Hector O'Halloran and his man, Mark Anthony O'Toole *(1843)*

52. Erin-Go-Bragh; or Irish Life Pictures *(1859)*

ANTHONY TROLLOPE

53. The Macdermots of Ballycloran *(1847)*

54. The Kellys and the O'Kellys *(1848)*

55. Castle Richmond *(1860)*

56. An Eye for an Eye *(1879)*

57. The Land-Leaguers *(1883)*

JOSEPH SHERIDAN LE FANU

58. The Purcell Papers with a Memoir by Alfred Perceval Graves *(1880)*

59. The Cock and Anchor: Being a Chronicle of Old Dublin City *(1845)*

60. The House by the Church-Yard *(1863)*

WILLIAM ALLINGHAM

61. Lawrence Bloomfield in Ireland. A Modern Poem *(1864)*

CHARLOTTE RIDDELL (MRS. J.H. RIDDELL)

62. Maxwell Drewitt *(1865)*

63. The Nun's Curse *(1888)*

T. MASON JONES

64. Old Trinity. A Story of Real Life *(1867)*

ANNIE KEARY

65. Castle Daly. The Story of an Irish Home Thirty Years Ago *(1875)*

MAY LAFFAN HARTLEY

66. Hogan, M. P. *(1876)*
67. Flitters, Tatters, and the Counsellor and Other Sketches *(1879)*

CHARLES JOSEPH KICKHAM

68. Knocknagow: or, the Cabins of Tipperary *(1879)*

MARGARET M. BREW

69. The Burtons of Dunroe *(1880)*
70. Chronicles of Castle Cloyne. Pictures of Munster Life *(1885)*

EMILY LAWLESS

71. Hurrish. A Study *(1886)*

72. With Essex in Ireland *(1890)*

73. Grania. The Story of an Island *(1892)*

74. Maelcho. A Sixteenth-Century Narrative *(1894)*

75. Traits and Confidences *(1898)*

WILLIAM O'BRIEN

76. When We Were Boys *(1890)*

ANONYMOUS

77. Priests and People: A No-Rent Romance *(1891)*